T0322522

THE COILED SERPENT

Also by Camilla Grudova:

The Doll's Alphabet
Children of Paradise

THE COILED SERPENT

CAMILLA GRUDOVA

atlantic·*fiction*

First published in hardback in Great Britain in 2023 by
Atlantic Books, an imprint of Atlantic Books Ltd.

Copyright © Camilla Grudova, 2023

2 3 4 5 6 7 8 9

A CIP catalogue record for this book is available from
the British Library.

Hardback ISBN: 9781838956356
EBook ISBN: 9781838956370

Printed and bound by CPI (UK) Ltd, Croydon CR0 4YY

Atlantic Books
An Imprint of Atlantic Books Ltd
Ormond House
26–27 Boswell Street
London
WC1N 3JZ

www.atlantic-books.co.uk

Contents

'I shall rage on raw meat'

Vladimir Mayakovsky

Through Ceilings and Walls

I travelled to the island – one of the largest and most isolated in the world – by boat, and arrived on a drizzly, humid morning. The island's government, in liaison with my university and my own government, had organised accommodation for me in a city not far from the purported site of some important Roman remains. I took a train there from the seaport, where they had confiscated my old maps and guide to their country, saying they were of no use anyway. They had, however, let me keep my small green edition of Homer's *Odyssey* in the original Ancient Greek. At the train station, I was able to buy tea in a grey paper cup, a small boiled potato wrapped in foil and a chocolate bar. There was no one else in the station except for an old woman wearing a lopsided wig, strands of her own white hair sticking out from underneath the brown curls. She was slowly eating a boiled egg with one hand and clutching a grey paper cup of tea with the other. The chocolate bar was pale and very sweet. It did not melt in my mouth, but stayed solid until I chewed it and swallowed it in waxy lumps.

My accommodation was in a terraced house built from the city's famous grey stone. It had large windows, one of which was blocked out with stone in the same pattern as the panes in the other windows. Many of the houses on the street also had this, some with more blocked stone windows than others.

My host was an older woman wearing a green tweed jacket and skirt. Stapled to the lapel of her jacket was a dried white flower. She wore a matching green hat, with plastic green eggs on it, and brown leather shoes. Her legs were bare even though it was cold. Our countries both spoke English, but it was hard to understand her, as every word sounded like a yawn. I stared at her mouth as she spoke. It was like there was something else in it besides her tongue, teeth, gums and tonsils. I imagined a strange growth in each of her cheeks, swollen and sore. There was wet snot in one of her nostrils and she dabbed it with a patterned hanky.

In the hall of the guest house there were framed grey etchings of whale and fox hunting, and a large painting of the Prime Minister. He wore a purple suit and tiny thick round spectacles. He was bald. He wore a white poppy on his suit lapel. I had seen paintings of him at the port where I arrived, and in the train station too. He had been Prime Minister of the island since long before I was born.

My landlady took me up to my room, using a torch, as the lamps above us were dim. She did not give me a tour of the rest of the house. The bedroom was sparsely decorated: a desk, an empty shelf and, taped to one of the walls, a picture, ripped from a newspaper, of a royal wedding from long ago. The bride's face and hands were blocked out with green crayon scribbles, which made it look like the prince was marrying an empty white dress. The bed frame was in a nook in the wall, and it was so tall there were steps leading up to it. The room had been fitted with two hotplates, an electric kettle, an antique-looking toaster, a radio, a small variety of pots and pans and tins which said 'Sugar', 'Coffee' and 'Tea' on them but, on closer inspection, were empty. It was clear the landlady intended me to cook in my room rather than in the kitchen. I asked about a fridge or freezer.

'We don't normally refrigerate eggs and such things,' she said, then pointed to the windowsill. 'But that will do for milk. It is quite cold here, even in summer.'

After she left me to unpack my things, I realised there was a chamber pot in the room. I did not know if it was for decoration or my use. She did not show me where the bathroom was, but I found one down the hall from my room that seemed little used. There was black mould on the walls, a clawfoot tub stained with rust, and a vase of dried roses beside the sink. The window was misted glass and there was a very ancient newspaper by the toilet. I did not know if it was meant for wiping or to read, but I took it to my room to read and made my way to find toilet paper at a nearby shop.

The window display of the only shop I found was wholly comprised of cuts of raw red meat, as if the meat were the tongue of the shop and the window was its mouth. Inside I found potatoes, Brussels sprouts, small apples, eggs, white bread, bottles of milk, a larger variety of meat, lollipops, boiled sweets, the same brand of chocolate I had purchased at the train station which didn't melt in the mouth, and spices in jars with orange lids. There were shelves and shelves of sweets, called Milk Chews, which came in white wrappers with a cow on. There were many of the same toy, a stuffed green wingless dragon or dinosaur with a long tail, and dolls with straw-blonde hair holding small national flags. These too were wrapped in plastic.

I was a vegetarian, as most people were in my country, so I avoided the cuts of meat. I bought apples, potatoes, eggs and a jar of peppercorns, along with a packet of coffee powder and some of the Milk Chews, out of curiosity. I had read that the inhabitants of the island only traded with one South Asian country, which led to their reliance on turmeric, pepper, curry powder, tea and coffee. It was a country they had once pillaged and claimed to own, and I suppose they had a certain violent pride in eating the spices from there. The coffee did not smell of coffee and the eggs were rotten inside.

At the guest house, I grabbed a pan and went to the bathroom to get water. It looked like there was a green olive stuck in the drain of the sink. I poured water from the tap on it to push it down, but it only quivered. I touched it – it was softer than an olive – and pressed on it. It quickly disappeared into the dark of the pipes.

When I returned I noticed a large porcelain jug in the room, filled with water. I suppose my landlady had filled it for me to prevent me from wandering to other parts of her house. I boiled the potatoes and ate them for supper with pepper. I found a copy of Beatrix Potter's *The Tale of Mr. Jeremy Fisher* in the room, and read it after my meal. I had given up on the newspaper I had found in the bathroom, as it only contained old royal gossip, recipes and children's stories. There was no news of the outside world. I hadn't seen any newspapers in the shops. I had an apple and some Milk Chews for dessert. The Milk Chews were beige squares that were hard to chew; I couldn't finish one, and I took it out of my mouth, leaving it on my bedside table with the apple core. I brushed my teeth using the water from the bathtub drain.

The next morning, I set out to find ruins. I was met at my lodgings by an old man who said he was an eminent historian. He wore a green jumper with brown stains on it, a grey blazer and a sagging leather satchel, which smelled. His face was covered in cuts and long hairs that had been missed by the razor; he had shaved it that morning, I suppose, in expectation of our meeting. He was accompanied by a young woman whose black hair was braided into a crown around her head. She dressed like my landlady, more or less, and was not introduced to me, though it was she who drove the eminent historian and me to the ancient site. Her car was a white Volkswagen Beetle, with thick wool blankets over the seats, which I found stifling in the humid morning.

They took me to the site of an ancient wall which divided the north and south of the country. I felt I couldn't dig around comfortably in front of them, so I waited until they were turned in another direction, chatting with the same overcrowded mouths as the landlady, then I crouched, my back turned to them, digging quickly with my hands. All I found was more dirt. I put some in my pocket, along with a stone. When I turned around, I saw the professor step on a large snail. He crushed it with his foot until it looked like a shattered teacup full of jelly. The woman giggled. It was a Roman snail, imported by the Romans, along with dormice, because they had liked to eat them.

When I returned to my lodgings, my landlady, waiting by the door, commented that my clothes were quite masculine, as was my short black hair. I said it was common in my country for both men and women to dress the way I did, and she said, 'Not here.'

Back in my bedroom, I took the soil and stone out of my pocket and wrapped them in cling film. I would take the bundle back to my country and do tests on it in my university's laboratory.

I woke up to find a long, floral dress on a hanger on my door, which had been opened an inch to hang it. I folded it – it smelled as if it had been worn long ago and not washed – and left it on a small chair in the hall.

The historian and his driver picked me up again, and took me on a city tour of bland government buildings, schools and nineteenth-century monuments of royals. I asked the historian about certain other sites I was intent on visiting – a bathhouse, a mosaic depicting fish and fruit, the remains of an amphitheatre – and how to get to them from where I was. He drew me a very vague map using his knee as a desk. When he handed it to me, I noticed the ink had leaked onto his trousers. I asked him about trains, and he shrugged and said he was driven everywhere.

I returned to my room, exhausted and disappointed, and examined the map the professor had given me. I decided I would leave in the morning, to take whatever train I could, wherever I could, to find more ancient sites. It was better than staying where I was. I put on my pyjamas.

I didn't want to eat. I developed a stomach ache and wind – from eating too many of the apples, I supposed – and my faeces that night reminded me of the green gelatinous substance I had seen in the drain, which filled me with the horrible thought that it had been faeces in the sink. Worried about my health, and too bewildered to seek medical attention, I pushed my excretion around the toilet bowl with a spoon from my room, which I vowed to remember by the tiny royal on its tip and return to the kitchen. I don't know what I sought: perhaps blood, or remnants of what I had eaten, but I was surprised when one of the pieces moved of its own accord and slid down the pipe. The others, less firm, crumbled as I touched them with the spoon, until they resembled pond algae.

There was another sound in the bathroom, coming from one of the plastic mousetraps that were all over the house, the kind like a miniature hallway with a door that locks once the mouse goes in. There were four in my bedroom alone. I had seen my landlady carrying three from elsewhere in the house to a bathroom. I had heard the toilet flush and she returned with the empty cages, their doors open, revealing speckles of mouse poo. The water pressure in the house was very bad; I couldn't imagine the mice being swallowed with one flush, and instead imagined them squeaking as they drowned in shallow water with no escape.

I went downstairs to get more water, holding my stomach, and the now filthy spoon.

My landlady was playing *Madame Butterfly* downstairs. It sounded off – something was wrong with the shrill voice of the singer – until I realised she was singing in English rather than Italian.

My landlady wasn't in the kitchen, but there was a gramophone in there I hadn't noticed before. I walked towards it to see the record label, which read 'Moira McKeller Sings Mrs Butterfly'. Around it were piles of commemorative royal plates from many, many years. All the crockery was in commemoration of different royal events: coronations, weddings, jubilees, their odd and ugly royal faces surrounded by leaves or gold braid.

I opened one of the drawers. Each piece of cutlery had a little royal face on the end. I put the filthy one in with the others.

On the table, there was roast chicken, herring and pigs' feet, left over in bowls covered with cloth. I peeled back the cloth, watched the skins gathering condensation. The walls were covered in shelves of jars of spices, and jars of jams and chutneys, a few bottles of what looked like homemade ketchup, dark brown and thick. There was some food left on a plate, with a fork and knife set down as if it were a meal to be returned to: grey slices of chicken slathered with strawberry jam.

I turned on the kitchen tap. Water didn't come out: something slimy and green did. Something was wrong with the plumbing, and my faeces was coming out of the kitchen sink. It did not stop coming out, there was so much – it was more than I alone could have produced, accompanied by hair and tiny bits of undigested food. I would have to leave the taps to run, until the slime cleared.

I thought I saw something move inside the gramophone's flaring horn, the same quivering green exuding I had seen in the sink, and backed away. There was a white and pale yellow growth on the pile of green coils in the sink, like the yolk of a partially cooked egg. There was no sign of water. I would break it open with a fork or knife. I took the fork off the plate of chicken, and as I moved closer, the smell became worse, the smell of old pipes, of everything swallowed by a drain. The growth moved, the top layer disappearing, revealing a dark gap of pupil. I could make no sense of its anatomy. Its body was everywhere, not just in the sink. It was in the pipes, the walls, the furniture. I was already in its stomach.

Ivor

We are all second, third or even fifth sons. We were sent to Wakeley Boarding School aged eight for Year Five and stayed on until Year Twenty. We didn't count how many years that was, or fully comprehend how much time constituted a year; we were just excited to go off to boarding school like our fathers and older brothers, to leave the nursery. We were disappointed not to go to the same school as our fathers and eldest brothers, but so were our sisters, who were not sent to school at all. We were given a brochure from Wakeley: there was an illustration of a beautiful, dark-haired boy playing rugby on the cover. Our nannies packed up our teddies and toys, photos of our families, shortbread and chocolate. Some of our nannies wept; we did not know why: we assumed we would see them again soon.

Wakeley was in the middle of the countryside. Which county, we couldn't say. Some of us remembered our fathers saying they were taking us to Derbyshire, others to Somerset, though a senior student with a passion for nature said based on the studies he did of animals and flora on the school grounds we were in Dumfries and Galloway, Scotland. The land surrounding the school was beautiful and hilly; the grounds so extensive we had no need to go beyond them. There was a stable with horses, a swimming pool, tennis courts, a library, a graveyard, a chapel and several dormitories, each with its own housemaster and tutors. We had advanced lessons: every year for biology, a zoo donated an elephant fetus for us to dissect and for months the specimens lay in tanks and jars of formaldehyde in our classroom like wrinkled old raincoats. There was a big grey computer that could do sums. Languages we could study ranged from Arabic to Russian.

As younger boys, we had to do tuck-shop runs for the seniors in our house who had their own rooms, a mark of their status. Chocolate bars, haemorrhoid cream, newspapers, boiled sweets, Gentleman's Relish, malted milk, cigarettes. One senior would cane us if his newspaper was wet. We didn't like the seniors and didn't understand how they could look like our fathers and grandfathers yet were still boys at school wearing the same striped ties and caps as us. The headmaster told us they were special boys who had a lot to learn before going out into the world, and that boys who entered the world too soon missed school and their friends terribly. We half forgot about these older students unless we were doing chores for them. We had our own classes, games, celebrations, clubs – the Cheese Club, the Ancient Rome Club, the French Club. The older boys blended into the antique furniture of our houses, red-faced and dusty like velvet armchairs, or spindly and brown like side tables.

As we got older and became seniors ourselves, we were dependent on those tuck-shop excursions, those moments of forced tenderness from the younger boys. We recognised the disappointment of a damp newspaper, pages stuck together, that as new, young boys we had not understood.

The main chore we had to do for the seniors was make toast and cut it into little pieces for them. We saw house tutors tie bibs around their necks for each meal and accompany them to the bathroom or push their wheel-chairs throughout the halls of Wakeley, cut their toenails in the evening and insert their false teeth in the morning. Our teachers told us it was gracious to help the elderly. We had to ignore the sounds of them soiling themselves in the halls, or when they pinched our bottoms, weeping as they did so, their own backsides sagging like abandoned bowls of porridge.

The boys in the fourteenth form who resembled our teachers and our half-forgotten fathers were still hearty and athletic. They didn't need our help and they ignored us completely. They had their own clubrooms where they drank and argued. Occasionally one would come into our dorms at night very drunk and the tutors had to chase them off using brooms and smiles. Sometimes they were so quiet that none of us, not even the tutors, heard them, and we would wake up in seething, mysterious pain to find one of them sleeping beside us, hulking and stinking.

Everyone competed to prepare toast for Ivor, a head boy and senior. He didn't look like any of the other seniors: he was still beautiful, he was still captain of the rugby team, played lacrosse, swam, sang and took part in all sorts of games.

He never asked for anything from the tuck shop but we brought him presents anyway. We learned that he liked rhubarb and custard sweets and disliked the newspapers – he never read them and rolled the pages into balls he threw at other boys, sometimes filled with flour so that those he hit were left with white faces like clowns.

Ivor was the only one we served toast whole to – he didn't need it quartered.

For breakfast, Ivor had toast with anchovy paste, a beef sausage split down the middle and filled with marmalade and a cup of tea with neither milk nor sugar.

He ate heartily of whatever was on offer for lunch and supper: steak pie with stew, boiled fish, roasts, kedgeree,

Wellington, rarebit, ham, puddings, and in later years, lasagne and curry, chips, baked potatoes and chilli.

Ivor had dark curly hair that never went grey, red lips, flushed cheeks and a pallor so powdery some of us thought he wore makeup.

The so-called 'makeup' did not come off or run in the shower or bath, nor did he sweat when he played sports.

When he was playing a rugby game, a few of us snuck into his room and ransacked it, looking for makeup or hair dye, but we didn't find any. In the drawers of his desk and under his mattress we found only old playing cards and a purple wrapper from a chocolate bar.

On his desk was an unopened Kendal mint cake, three Rupert annuals and his Greek books, a cup full of pens, a tin of rusty pen nibs and a jar of blue ink, a paper bag of stale penny sweets shaped like bottles and babies. He only wrote with dark blue ink and we imitated him. Most of the teachers could not tell the difference between dark blue and black, but we could.

Above his desk he had a picture of the Queen. When the Queen died, the image was replaced by a picture of the King, then later another king, and then a queen again. No one knew where the old pictures ended up. They were always in the same frame.

He had piles of sports things: a pig's bladder football, wooden tennis rackets and lacrosse sticks made with sheep intestine webbing, yellowing cricket pads. On his bed was a dirty teddy bear with a crooked face named Bombozine. In between Bombozine's legs were badly sewn stitches holding a hole together. There were milk stains on the legs, the fur stiff and bunched together.

He had a small taxidermy crocodile, mounted on his wall, and a wooden African mask. These items were a source of wonder to us.

When we first arrived at Wakeley we copied the way Ivor did everything until his habits came naturally to us. His way of pushing back his hair when reading, or humming as he tied his shoes, the way he wrapped his wool scarf around his neck and used words like 'ripping' and 'first rate' and the Scots word 'blether'. We soon called him Ivy. Some of us bought red lipstick from the tuck shop and wore it as we got older and our natural boyish colours faded.

The toilets at Wakeley were unreliable, with cracked wooden seats, and rarely flushed properly. We would often judge each other's defecations by size and shape. Once, a boy using the bathroom after Ivor discovered a perfectly white piece of faeces, like crushed wet chalk. It smelled of nothing. He said it reminded him of a cloud. Like most of us, Ivor did not like to take baths or showers because the water was lukewarm. Our hair was greasy, our bottoms as dirty and cracked as those of stray cats. We rolled in mud on the grounds and spilled mashed potato, snot and puddings on our uniforms.

Every term a man would come to inspect everyone's hair for lice. He had a black comb which he kept in a jar of blue liquid and carefully brushed each boy's head, wearing a pair of magnifying spectacles. He was very tall and thin with a pot belly. His own head was shaven, except for a white wisp over one ear. He complained to the headmaster if he found too much dandruff, saying the boys needed to have their hair washed more often.

Though Ivor's hair always appeared to be clean and well brushed, he had the most bugs in his hair. Each time the inspector came he would find fleas, bedbugs, ticks, little white worms, dozens of eggs, and Ivor would be prescribed a foul-smelling pink shampoo we never saw him use. The inspector seemed to enjoy combing through Ivor's hair; almost every strand of hair was covered in black insects.

The man squeezed the bugs between his fingers then dropped them on the towel positioned beneath his inspecting stool where the boys sat. One boy, Clive, who was more infatuated with Ivor than most, grabbed one of the bugs that was still alive; he cradled it in his hands and took it to his room where he put it in an old cigar box he had stolen from a senior. Unoriginally, he named it Ivor.

Clive fed the bug bits of sweets and cake and drops of his own blood by pricking his finger with the tip of his fountain pen. It grew very fat and soon became the size of a guinea pig, and he got a bigger box to put it in. It gave off a sickly sweet smell from the food Clive gave it. It was round and brown in colour with bits of black, as shiny as the polished wooden floors in our dorms, the ridges in its shell resembling the cracks between the boards. It had six furry legs and a pair of pincers.

He had read in a magazine about flea circuses and tried to teach the creature tricks. He trained it to jump through a ring and climb a set of steps he made from toy blocks and rubbers.

'Please don't tell Ivor or any of the teachers about my darling pet,' he begged us, and we didn't, as there seemed something disgusting about Clive's care of the bug and we didn't want to be associated with it, though we still went into his bedroom to watch it do tricks, and to stroke its hard back. Pets were not allowed, except one Headmaster had for a time – a vizsla named Brutus, whom we all loved, although he would often pin us to the ground and hump us because he wasn't fixed.

One morning Clive didn't come down to breakfast. The housemaster went to wake him and found him lying in bed, underneath the covers, the bug where his face should have been. The housemaster knocked it off with an iron poker. Where the bug had sat was a sort of bloody indent of what it had eaten of Clive's face; it had taken a big bite out of his head like an oozy pudding. The housemaster killed the bug using the coal poker, then the housekeepers burned the bug and buried Clive. The sheets were stained with blood that couldn't be washed out: Wakeley was mean with money (many families stopped paying tuition but Wakeley never threw a boy out) so every fortnight a new boy was given Clive's old bloody sheets, faded to a brown. Some were so scared of sleeping on them that they would jump into another boy's bed. Others said that Clive's housemaster didn't kill the bug at all and it was still wandering the pipes and halls of Wakeley and would eat our feet. All of us started to wear our leather rugby shoes to bed and did so for the rest of our lives, though we were not sure how long a bug lived.

We had a memorial for Clive in our main hall. Ivor sang a hymn in his beautiful sweet voice. It felt like he was not just singing for Clive, but for all of us, past and present. The choirmaster often said, 'Ivor's voice is made of marble, not plaster,' and we were all jealous of Clive who, in his death, received a song from Ivor. Some of us jumped from the Wakeley roofs in the hope of dying, but merely ended up with broken arms and legs. The school put giant nets around the façade of Wakeley, to catch us when we jumped, and eventually the craze for jumping stopped, though the teachers kept the nets up and they soon seemed like they had always been there.

There was one year Ivor wasn't in the class photos decorating our halls, or in the calligraphic lists which, before photographs, detailed that year's students. We wondered a lot about this lost year. Some said he was overseas, fighting in a colonial war to which all Wakeley students were conscripted. They said that he was the only survivor, and that was where the African mask and crocodile came from. Others said he was in the Hebrides, staying with a relative who was ill, and that he inherited the mask and crocodile from them.

A very senior boy told us he had run away to Europe and had a woman, but we did not believe him. Ivor was only a boy. He showed no interest in women, only sports and lessons and friendship, we said. The senior boy showed us a black and white photo of a woman wearing only her brassiere and said it was Ivor's wife, but that it was a secret and we mustn't tell Ivor we knew. The thought was so horrid that we were sick and cried.

Occasionally boys ran away from Wakeley, and even, it was rumoured, got married and had children, but they always came back. They missed the food, their cosy dormitories, their routines, their friends and, most of all, Ivor.

They tried to find their families but could not locate their estates or anyone with the same name; we were all assigned last names similar in tone and status to our original names when we first started at Wakeley and it did not take long for us to forget what we used to be called.

Roddy, a year ahead of us, retained a clear image of his family's estate; not just the building but the surrounding trees and lakes. He missed it so much, he ran away from Wakeley and he found it, but the house was gone, torn down, replaced with multiple flats. He came back to Wakeley and said he wished he'd never left, as the house would have always existed then. He drowned himself in the school's swimming pool.

Our dorms were freezing. We filled our beds with heated bricks, hot-water bottles, stuffed toys, scarves, coats, socks. One boy even stole a teapot from the dining table over supper and lay huddled against it all night: he woke up to find his sheets all brown and the teapot cracked. Ivor never got cold. He let us huddle around him in his house common room, as if he were a fireplace, and read to us from his Rupert annuals, though his body gave off no heat, which we noticed when in contact with him on the rugby field.

Once, long ago on a June celebration, the one time our families came to visit, a woman in wool stockings with a heavy, hideous face like a bundle of rusty steel wool, so unlike Ivor's, came to watch him and the other boys row in the river, their heads decorated in flower crowns. She gave him a homemade walnut cake in a large round tin before she left. None of us had asked about the woman or talked to her, we were too excited to see our own families, and spent the night after they left weeping in our beds, on a blanket of smashed carnations and roses.

Whenever a cake was eaten at Wakeley, it was tradition to scream while it was being cut – to keep the devil away, the headmaster said. You could tell, from the screams, who had hit puberty already and who was still a little boy. Ivor's scream was the highest of all, as sharp and shiny as the knife itself.

Ivor didn't eat the walnut cake himself but distributed slices to other boys, in particular the ones who wouldn't stop weeping after their families left. A few of us thought this was suspicious, others generous. Those of us who got a slice of the cake waited in anticipation for something to happen, for us to die from poisoning, our stomachs in twists of agony, for our faces to become as beautiful as Ivor's, but it was only a normal cake, not even homemade but shop-bought from Fuller's. The sweetness of it made us stop crying. The woman only came once; we never saw her again. Ivor did not seem upset, and instead charmed everyone else's parents and siblings and cousins. Our families all said they were so glad we were at school with a nice boy like Ivor.

None of the seniors became teachers or headmasters at Wakeley; our teachers came from elsewhere. Some stayed all of their lives, others only a few months. If they had families, they lived off campus and drove in, going home on the weekends. At night and on lunch breaks, we broke into their cars and pretended to drive places. Many boys thought it unfair they could not become teachers at Wakeley, even after forty years of perfect grades in Latin, biology and Greek, their knowledge surpassing that of our teachers, but the headmaster said all the students were still boys.

Most of the seniors could only manage table tennis or chess in terms of games. Their lessons resembled those of the youngest boys: painting, reading, simple grammar, adding and subtracting. They were allowed brandy in the evening, and wine or ale with supper and lunch. They wore the same uniforms as us, with house scarves, though they also had spectacles, canes and protruding moles. When one graduated, we held a memorial for him in the main hall, his grades and prize medals placed on display for all to see, and we sang the Wakeley school song in his honour. The other seniors always wept, except Ivor. He said they had all had a jolly good time together and they would see each other again someday. We had to pack up the bags and possessions of seniors from our own house who'd graduated. We found badly written poems about Ivor in the backs of textbooks, and old photographs of other seniors, once young, with their arms around Ivor on the rugby pitch.

Once, we found an old brochure for Wakeley, wrinkled and yellow. It had a different font and a different year printed on it than the one we had received, but the picture was the same – a beautiful black-haired boy, Ivor; but such things were soon forgotten because the real Ivor was there among us.

On laundry day, all the boys gathered their sheets and pillowcases, their pants and their trousers, their names sewn onto the labels of each item, and threw their washing down the stairs of their houses for the cleaners to collect. The linens and uniforms billowed down like ghosts; the dirty pants fluttered onto the bannisters like shot birds and all the boys laughed if the cotton was soiled. Every time, in his own house, Ivor would jump down the stairs with the laundry and float down, landing gracefully on his bottom and laughing. We all knew that if we were to do the same, we would smash our skulls. We gathered that perhaps Ivor was light as a bed sheet, made clean over and over again to comfort us in our sleep.

Description and History
of a British Swimming Pool/
Banya Banya!

There was a sign on the door of the Victoria Swim Centre and Turkish Baths which said:

No coughs

No open wounds

No nightgowns

The building was made of beefy red brick on the outside, with skylights emerging out of the centre top like blisters on roasted flesh.

It contained pools ranging from cold to hot, the Turkish rooms, a Russian sauna, a weightlifting gym and – since many of the surrounding houses did not have showers or baths themselves, only a single sink and a toilet – it also had baths and showers. The residents came every week with chunky bottles of cologne, big brown and yellow and orange soap bars, and green bottles of medicated shampoo.

It was the largest pool complex of its kind in the United Kingdom and was opened by its namesake, Queen Victoria, who praised it for bringing hygiene, health and cleanliness to the population, an issue close to her dear Albert's heart. The Victoria Swim Centre and Turkish Baths was built surrounding an ancient Roman bath, which still existed in some unknown part of the complex and which some pool-goers desperately tried to find, believing it was a place of orgies and indulgence, where there were grapes and children.

The pool centre had a special swimsuit designed for Queen Victoria, a complex and modest frilled black costume of rubber and cotton with a matching cap. At the pool opening, she was briefly submerged, like a diving-bell spider, or enormous dark floating turd, before being pulled out by her servants.

The swimming costume was now on display, in a glass box, in the foyer of the pool complex's entrance, which also contained a shop where one could buy more modern swimming gear: rubber caps with daisies and seashells on them, goggles, orange and green armbands, rings shaped like flamingos and swans, blow-up crocodiles and whales, Speedos, flippers, towels, wool caps for the sauna. There were bathing costumes to rent, all the same drab pale pink, from Speedos to bikinis with 'property of Victoria Swim Centre' written on the inner label. There was a dark brown and orange vending machine which sold two kinds of soup in plastic cups: chicken, which was bright yellow, and beef, which was pale red.

The president of the pool centre was a woman with large shoulders, Iona MacDougal, who wandered around with a whistle around her neck and a faceless dummy torso under her arm. She wore a rough, old-fashioned swimsuit which covered her legs to her knees.

She was a former Olympic champion swimmer and her hair was thin and crisp from years of chlorine and salt submersion. She was famous for accidentally breaking the neck of another woman on her synchronised swimming team, before becoming a multiple gold-medal winner in women's freestyle races.

The torso, along with Jemima – a beautiful porcelain doll wearing a blue silk gown – were tools to train lifeguards. They had to rescue them from all the different pools, a test only a small minority of lifeguards passed.

The sea pool was salt water rather than chlorine, and it had rocks, seaweed, sand and fishes in it. There was a large metal and canvas contraption on the deep edge of the pool which a lifeguard had to crank to create waves. The harder they did so, the bigger the waves would be.

There was also a freshwater pool, which imitated a swift-flowing English river and was home to many frogs and lily pads. This pool always had two lifeguards watching it because it drew in suicidal young ladies of a romantic nature. Nightgowns and dresses were banned from the pools as such women usually wore them, not wanting to end their lives in a bikini.

There was a diving pool, whose floor could move up and down to make it deep as a cathedral was tall.

There were hot bubbly pools, ice-dip pools which relaxed the muscles, and lukewarm pools full of bits of dead skin. Once every six months the staff released a bunch of fishes into it to clean it by eating all the skin, then scooped them out again, putting them in a tank in the office.

Some of the pools were too old to have a proper drainage system, and it was much cheaper to use the fishes than have one installed.

The Turkish rooms contained a tiny ice pool, red velvet fainting chairs and armchairs to lie on, a tepidarium (warm room), a caldarium (hot room) and a steam room, which was dark with brown and beige tiles.

The door to the steam room had a tiny window in it; you could see steam and sometimes a sweating head. It was dark and steamy inside. Sometimes you would brush against the thigh or hand of another person, and more often than not, those thighs and hands were one of the many mushrooms that grew in the steam room, feeding on human sweat, because the steam room was rarely cleaned. Some of the mushrooms were the size of children. The tiles were loose, and if you peeled one off the wall, a fleshy and furry interior was revealed.

The Russian sauna was made of wood and had birch switches for bathers to slap themselves with. It was rarely used as it was home to a tiny hairy man with long fingernails and toenails who threw the buckets of hot water on whoever entered.

There were men who went directly from the Turkish baths to the big pools without showering, and the water turned grey around them. They jumped into the ice bath, their moustaches instantly becoming frosted. The water was filled with ice cubes with bits of grey skin in them.

Iona's pregnancy was said to be the reason she'd had to retire from Olympic competition. Most of the staff of the swim centre said she got impregnated by a beluga whale while swimming off the coast of Canada, and that's why her son was so smooth and round. His name was Harold-Ivan, and his father was a Soviet swimmer. Everyone called him Whaletard. Most days he wandered around the pool in a pair of beige swimming trunks and a red lifesaver sitting over his belly: he did not know how to swim, though he had been taking lessons for all of his nineteen years. He sat in the sauna for long periods, sucking his thumb, or watched people change in the changing rooms. He was hairless except for one long hair growing out of his left shoulder.

Iona was more attached to her giant tortoise, who had a nest under her office desk and followed her around the pools. He liked to bite children's arms. She fed him on expensive imported fruit: mangosteens, pineapple, papayas, along with green cabbages. Iona lived off egg salad sandwiches and artichoke liquor, a bottle of which she kept on her desk with a teacup to pour it into. Every day she made an egg salad sandwich for herself, and a ham one for Harold-Ivan as eggs gave him wind.

The lifeguards employed at the Victoria Swim Centre got to sit on high chairs overlooking the pools, reading novels, wearing yellow outfits, while the junior lifeguards had to clean. There were balls of hair, grey skin, toenails, soiled underwear and nappies, water-sodden sanitary towels, hairbands, dentures, crushed spectacles, faeces, plasters, false teeth and real teeth, scabs, a man's full black beard as if torn off his face, oily forgotten swimming caps, lost swimming badges, tapeworms.

A man came in every week and washed himself with a jar of mayonnaise and a bottle of apple cider vinegar. The mayonnaise mixed with his hair clogged the drains and they had to fill the drains with chemicals while wearing rubber gloves and gas masks to do so.

There was a girl with a large patch of hair on the back of one of her thighs and she brushed it in the shower using a pink child's comb. A blind man who came swimming once a week wore goggles to protect his glass eyes, but the goggle suction pulled them out and the lifeguards had to retrieve them from various places. Harold-Ivan coveted these glass eyes, and when he found them he put one in his belly button, the other down his swimming trunks.

When the pool was shut the lifeguards had to tie sponges to their hands and feet and dive into the pools and scrub away the green-black and brown algae, and feed the fishes and frogs in the sea and river pools.

They had to clean the rental bathing suits and hang them up to dry for the next day's use.

The pool that the lifeguards were all afraid of was one with a thick canvas cover attached to the pool with metal hooks, which had rusted. It was so tightly bound it was like a giant water bed. Something underneath the canvas moaned and the cloth rippled now and again.

They were told to look underneath one day when Harold-Ivan disappeared and they slashed the canvas with a knife, only to find the rippled and barnacled texture of a whale's skin. Harold-Ivan was found outside the Russian sauna, covered in burns. He was wrapped up in bandages by Iona and resembled an earthworm more than a mummy.

He continued to wander around the pools, and his bandages became damp and sodden, the skin underneath custardy. Pimples and cysts sprouted around the vicinities of his burns. His one hair grew back white and crinkled. Before his wounds were healed he went back into the Russian sauna where he was found sucking the tiny red penis of the little bearded man who was always in there.

Iona put a lock on the Russian sauna. Customers had to ask for a key at the front desk and wear it around their neck or ankle while they were at the pool centre.

Every Sunday the biggest pool was filled with an inflatable canvas castle for children to play on; it was designed to look like one of Queen Victoria's castles and had been given to the pool on the fiftieth anniversary of its opening. It had faded peacocks, horses, vines and a youthful Prince Albert on it. The lifeguards could never prevent a man with long legs that splashed all over the place and long oily slick hair from swimming around it like a shark. He was too quick for them to catch. The canvas castle was very old and had slits in it that children sometimes disappeared into. They would still be lost by the time the castle was deflated and put away for the night, and there was a whole group of them that just lived inside, eating the old sweat and slime on its inner walls. Sometimes they walked out again the next time it was inflated, but usually they were too terrified of the sound of the banging against the sides and bottom of the castle to ever return.

The Custard Factory

The explosion happened one mid-morning at the Swan Custard Factory. A dust-cloud of cornflour was ignited, blowing off the roof of the building, injuring nine workers and killing one. When the fire engines arrived, the water they used to put out the fire turned to custard when mixed with all the powder and heat. It flowed down the neighbouring streets, where it was eaten by pigeons and little children who ran out after it with teacups to fill.

One unfortunate girl started to choke after drinking two cups of the liquid. Her father pounded her stomach until she threw up two human teeth, a fingernail and a blue stud earring shaped like a butterfly. These had belonged to Gloria-Jean Lewis, the one casualty of the explosion.

The owner of the factory was Alfred Swan III, grandson of the original Alfred Swan, a pharmacist who had invented instant egg-free custard powder after his wife had an allergic reaction at a dinner party. The original Alfred Swan and his wife were unsure which was the offending ingredient until she fainted and broke out in a rash a few days later after eating a boiled egg. No one knew what had caused her to suddenly be unable to stomach eggs. An untold part of the story, absent from the official histories of the custard company, is that she subsequently ate a whole jar of pickled eggs in an attempt to kill herself. She was found by her husband beside the empty jar, and was sent to an institution where staff were given strict instructions not to feed her any eggs, or place any eggs in her surroundings.

The custard powder made in Alfred Swan's factory was simply cornflour, yellow colouring and a little flavouring to make it look and taste a bit eggy. The instructions suggested it could be mixed with either milk or water. It was mainly sold in bulk to boarding schools where children were hit, and to little corner shops where it sat on dusty shelves, and was bought by old men who had gone to such schools, craving the desserts of their childhood.

The air around the factory smelled sweet, as did the houses of the factory workers, their clothes and hair always covered in a light layer of custard dust. Most of the workers took extra custard powder home: the stuff they swept off the floors into paper bags, the batches that weren't the exact shade of pale yellow for which the brand was famous.

The office of the custard factory was decorated with china swan figurines, and a large swan egg on a brass stand. There was a giant painting of the original Alfred Swan, but none of his wife. Her drawings of eggs were lost to time. The institution had closed down long ago.

Gloria-Jean, who was named after a 1950s actress she didn't care for, had joined the factory when she was twenty-one. She had long red hair she had to keep in a hairnet on shift, like something bloody caught in a spider's web, and she was the only staff member who didn't bring any custard home, because it gave her diarrhoea. She liked to read Shakespeare and Margaret Cavendish. There was a man, perhaps sixty or seventy years old, tall and stooped with wispy long white hair under a red baseball cap, who sat across from her every day while she ate her lunch in the staff canteen. He mixed whatever custard powder he had swept off the floors that morning into a cup of black tea (he had his own dainty, floral mug) and drank it with an absent smile on his face. Every day, he brought a sandwich: two slices of white bread that appeared to have nothing in between them.

Gloria-Jean eventually learned that there was a very thinly spread layer of mayonnaise inside. The man loved mayonnaise more than anything else in the world, and carefully rationed it day by day. Gloria-Jean ate rotten, wrinkly apples, brown grapes, cold baked beans she spooned straight from the can, uncooked noodles from Chinese supermarkets, raw potatoes, boxes of cream biscuits. She didn't like to cook. She only liked what she vaguely called her Mind's Work, which involved reading lots of public library books, looking at old things in secondhand shops and occasionally seeing a movie if it met certain mysterious criteria she couldn't explain.

One lunchtime, the old man passed her a cracked black and white photo he kept in a plastic Ziploc bag. It showed a young soldier in uniform, with light curls, a handsome face and many medals on his chest. The old man pointed at the photograph, then pointed at his own chest. He undid the first few buttons of his Swan Custard Factory uniform (a peach-coloured boiler suit with a tiny swan embroidered on the front pocket) to reveal a sweatshirt with the same medals – the ribbons wrinkled – pinned to his chest.

After work, he took her to a diner called the Café Mars. He ordered a blueberry muffin, and Gloria-Jean a plate of French fries. He eyed the little container of mayonnaise they gave her on the side, and she pushed it over to him. He spread it on his muffin. His name, he told her, was Wilfred Lewis.

Wilfred Lewis lived in a large brick house, painted pink. The garden was wild with roses and gnome figurines who had lost their shine and stood sadly like shrunken and bloated Greek statues. It was the house he was born in, and where he had lived, after the war, with his mother, until she died. The house did not have a washing machine or a fridge or any other modern appliances, though it had a fancy wooden and metal icebox, a toilet with a pull chain and an odd sort of bathtub with panelling around it, cracked with black mould.

There were lots of old and interesting things to admire in the house: hat boxes, very old rusted mousetraps, children's books about rag dolls and mermaids, china and porcelain figurines shaped like animals. Gloria-Jean thought the house contained a china figurine for every animal in the world – even the extinct ones, for she found a dodo. There are lots of old things for me to sort through and entertain myself with, she thought. That and the public library should keep me with things to do. And so she moved in with Wilfred Lewis, and later married him, so she would have some claim to the house.

She took Wilfred's mother's old room, which was the largest, with floral-print wallpaper and cupboards full of old cotton nighties. Wilfred continued to sleep in the room he'd always slept in, his old soldier's uniform and other war essentials in a suitcase under his bed. The only modern addition to the room was a poster of Garfield.

Gloria-Jean kept all of her books in a locked suitcase in her room. She did not want Wilfred to read them, or to look at the covers.

She took Wilfred Lewis's photograph from him, removed it from its plastic bag and put it in an elaborate silver frame she had bought at an antique shop. She placed it on her bedside table. She never looked at it, but she no longer wanted him to have it, in case he might show it to other young women, in delis, grocers' and at the park. She could tell Wilfred Lewis was displeased when she took the photograph from him, but he did not try to take it back.

In addition to her books and a few flimsy white polyester dresses she wore when not in her work uniform, Gloria-Jean brought an oil painting of her great-grandfather wearing a fur hat and the blue military uniform of a country that no longer existed. In order to get the painting out of his country, Gloria-Jean's grandfather had hidden it under his coat, pressed up against his back, padded with cloth. He pretended to be a hunchback. Because of this, they were eligible for a charitable fund from a church in their new country, but it meant that her grandfather had to wear the painting and the padded cloth under his coat whenever he left the house, in case the church people saw him. Over the years the painting became damaged from being worn outside so often, and from the nervous sweat of Gloria-Jean's grandfather.

Gloria-Jean and Wilfred Lewis had three children: Geoffrey, Ambrosia and Simon. Gloria-Jean named the first, Geoffrey, after a character from a novel she loved, but left the naming of the other two to Wilfred: she realised it was a mistake to name her children after beloved characters in fiction. Ambrosia was a rival brand of custard, and Gloria-Jean wept at Wilfred's lack of imagination.

Wilfred bought a television for the children on which they watched *The NeverEnding Story*, *Peter Pan*, multiple versions of *Robin Hood*, and a film called *The Last Unicorn*, which made Wilfred cry. Gloria-Jean would never sit down to watch television with her family, but sometimes she would stand at the door of the living room and watch snippets of the movie, then disappear.

Wilfred Lewis cooked for the children: custard with sliced hot dogs or pieces of grapes and melon, mayonnaise and sliced cheese sandwiches, macaroni with custard baked with potato chips on top. He took them to unpleasant zoos where tigers were kept in small cages, to the cinema for popular children's movies, to amusement parks. He bought them bags of plastic dinosaurs, guns and baby dolls.

Gloria-Jean lost interest in the children when one after the other cried when she put an interesting Victorian toy she'd found in some crevice of the house in their faces – a dusty monkey with no eyes holding a drum, a doll whose pink skin was cracked, a story book about goblins. The only objects of their grandmother's they liked were the animal figurines, many of which became chipped from being boisterously played with. Gloria-Jean carefully put them back together with glue. This activity, which required a lot of squinting, along with her reading, led her to need glasses.

After they graduated from school, all three children got jobs at the Swan Custard Factory and continued to live at home.

Geoffrey was the shortest, and Simon the tallest, which could only be put down to an improvement in school lunches, because the Lewis family always ate the same things, and did not change their habits much. They took to keeping many cats, which they fed with custard powder mixed with cold milk and kibble. To the family they were known as Whiskers, Pussy, Marmalade and Tiger, but Gloria-Jean had secret names for the cats, derived from botany books and Elizabethan drama, which she'd whisper in their ears when they slept on her bed. Sometimes she'd buy them the sweets she never bought for her children. One cat died from eating a chocolate bar, though she did not know that this was the cause of its death.

Geoffrey and Ambrosia had red hair like their mother, while Simon looked exactly like Wilfred Lewis.

When he became a teenager, Geoffrey dyed his hair black, pierced his own nose, putting a small gold earring of his mother's through it, and gave himself tattoos using a ballpoint pen and a razor. Simon liked to play baseball, and collected baseball cards. There was a type of children's chewing gum that imitated the chewing tobacco which famous baseball players consumed, and this was the only thing Simon liked to eat. He did not know that he wasn't supposed to swallow gum.

Ambrosia admired the swan egg in the factory office and wanted one just like it, so Alfred Swan made a deal with her that if she slept with him she could have it. He spent a long time moving his fingers around inside her as if he had lost something like a coin in her body. He did it so forcefully the whole room rattled and Ambrosia worried the swan egg would break. That was all he did. He cleaned his hand very carefully afterwards with a tissue and asked her if it had given her any pleasure. She said no, and took the swan egg off its brass stand.

She put it in her rucksack and finished her shift. By the time she was home, the egg had cracked into pieces. It must have been bumped by her co-workers in the locker room, gathering their things or changing out of their uniform.

She went into her mother's room, where Gloria-Jean spent her free hours reading with a hot-water bottle under her head, and asked her mother to fix the egg. Gloria-Jean took the pieces from her daughter and stared at them, knowing something dreadful and dramatic had happened.

Soon afterwards, Alfred Swan had installed a new swan egg in the exact same place, and Ambrosia realised that the precious object was not unique, though she did not know where to get one herself. Gloria-Jean saw the new egg too, and shivered with a vision of the future: a long line of broken swan eggs brought to her by her daughter, for her to piece together with glue.

Gloria-Jean resolved to set something in Alfred Swan's office on fire. She bought a plastic lighter from a corner shop. It was purple, with the outline of a Ninja Turtle imprinted on it. In an idle moment, wondering how a swan egg burned, she flicked it on and off when she was supposed to be sweeping the factory floor.

Once they were released from hospital, Geoffrey, Ambrosia, Wilfred Lewis and Simon all had to wear cloth bandages that they were required to change regularly. A burn of the degree they suffered does look like custard stuck to the skin. As the burns healed and dried, they peeled off the yellow skin and put it into a designated pot from which Wilfred Lewis shooed the cats away so they wouldn't eat the skin scraps.

Ambrosia liked to stick their animal figurines in the icebox, and when they were cold enough, place them against her burns.

The Green Hat

'Nothing like a tin of Bird's.'

The chemist opened the tin at the table and poured hot water into it from a kettle on an iron plate, stirring it and eating it with a spoon. He didn't eat it with cake or stewed fruit. 'Alfred Bird was an admirable chemist,' he said.

He threw the rest of the can out: he liked it to be opened fresh, though it was only cornflour with a bit of colouring.

Separately, and in different courses, he also had beef, and custard creams, which Angelica, his maid, had to bring from the kitchen on covered porcelain plates. Angelica didn't like the look of custard creams: the lettering on top of the biscuit spelling out 'CUSTARD CREAMS' looked like it had been written there by a child with a sewing needle.

The chemist always had his cook make boiled Brussels sprouts and cabbage, and Yorkshire puddings, which

Angelica also had to serve, but he did not eat them. He just liked to have them at the table for the appearance of a traditional meal. He told the cook to throw them out. The cook never did, but kept them for himself. He started to give bits and pieces to Angelica after she had worked there for a while and was trusted not to snitch. The cook was very windy from all the Brussels sprouts and cabbages.

Angelica hated to clean the cook's room, which had pictures of jockeys and horses torn out of newspapers taped to the walls, and green, flowerless plants in garish pots with dogs painted on them that she had to dust. In one of his drawers, she found a rubber doll which fitted into the palm of her hand. It jiggled like blancmange when she picked it up. It had blonde hair, also made of rubber, no clothes and it smelled.

Once the cook raged at her for throwing out an old fish and chips box which still had morsels in it.

She only took the Yorkshire puddings from the cook. The rest she flushed down the toilet because the chemist liked to cover everything in his rubbish bins and those of his neighbours with rat poison and she did not want the rats to suffer. Angelica ate the leftover Yorkshire puddings for breakfast, though they were clammy and soft like the skin of a hairless armpit. She had a small jar of red jam to dip the pieces in. Her bedroom was in the basement, beside the kitchen. The chemist's study was directly above, and she could hear him walking to and fro, plotting up new chemical recipes.

Her bed was very large and grand and took up most of the room. It was the old bed of the chemist and his wife, and very lumpy and stained. She felt so repulsed by it that she slept with her coat and other clothes spread out beneath her so she wouldn't have to touch the sheets. Her coat and her clothes were rattier, and dirtier, but they were her own.

At night she pushed her armchair and bedside table in front of her door. It rattled every night at 1.30 a.m. She could not tell if this was the cook or the chemist.

She had to wear a traditional maid's outfit: a black dress with a white apron and hat. She was only given one. At night, before bed, she scrubbed the armpits of the dress clean with soap and water and hung it in front of her fireplace, which was weakly lit with the small amount of coal the chemist allowed her.

The tiles around the fireplace were wispily painted with jolly-looking labouring peasants.

The chemist was the owner of Ambrosia Chemists Ltd, which had developed a green dye made with copper that turned out to be poisonous. A doctor discovered this and published a paper on it after his four children died from the wallpaper in their nursery; a design of frogs and fairies on lily pads. The green dye, which had been used for wallpaper, clothes, artwork, furniture fabric and toys, among other things, was banned. The government gave Ambrosia Chemists Ltd a large bailout, which increased the wealth of the chemist considerably. Realising poison was something he was good at, he invented a chemical that turned food poisonous after its best-before date. It stopped the starving from rooting through the bins of restaurants and grocers', and increased the profits of food companies as consumers threw out the products out of fear days before the expiry date, and bought more. Ambrosia Ltd had made deals with meat and dairy companies, chocolate factories, fruit distributors, bakeries, egg farms, small fudge shops and more. The products containing expiry poison were required to have a small sticker in the shape of a green pig's skull (a requirement Ambrosia Ltd were lobbying to get rid of) but the public were so frightened that they even threw out food without the tiny green skull.

All the windows of the house had iron bars over them to protect from thieves. In the chemist's study there was a large rhinoceros head mounted on the wall. It was one of Angelica's jobs to polish it.

Little flakes of the skin came off when she did. She carefully glued them back on like eighteenth-century beauty spots.

In the chemist's bedroom, there were large ferns in Chinese pots and a stuffed crocodile on top of the dresser with swampy brown skin. Its teeth were painted white, its mouth an unnatural bright red. The chemist's wife was on holiday in Italy indefinitely, and their children were at boarding school.

Angelica had to clean the children's bedrooms though they were only briefly there in the summer. The rooms were full of toys; the daughter had life-size dolls with moveable jaws, and a rocking horse painted blue and gold.

When cleaning she found old biscuits hidden in toy boxes, vulgar drawings of naked people, and a dead mouse swaddled in a hanky.

She put it all in a bin bag, along with a toy seal that smelled mildewy and was covered in spilt milk stains, and took them outside. By the bins, she saw a white and orange cat drooling. Dropping the bag of children's rubbish, she picked it up and brought it into her room.

She opened the cat's mouth and force-fed it sodium bicarbonate until it vomited up a collection of meat and fish covered in the distinctive powder that was the chemist's Vermin Kill poison. It was the same shade as his green dye: instead of discontinuing its manufacture when it was banned, he rebranded it as a household poison. It looked like mould, and was often mistaken as such by very hungry people looking for a crust of bread in someone else's waste ('A little mould won't hurt, just scrape it off with a knife'). Or perhaps they didn't care it was poison, they were so famished. She believed that sometimes the chemist went to the shops, bought fish, bread and other things, which he sprinkled with his own invention and put directly into the rubbish, because his heart was cruel. She named the cat Ludwig, after Beethoven.

Angelica's indulgence, besides black tea, was going to see a concert on her one evening off. She liked the bombastic symphonies of Beethoven most of all. Angelica used to have a husband who hated the symphony because the only seats they could afford did not have enough room for his long limbs and he always sat scowling, his limbs in awkward positions like an injured spider, his thin hands over his ears. He told her he didn't like music written twenty or fifty or a hundred years previously, and that concerts were for the bourgeoisie.

She stole pieces from an unused tea set from the kitchen for the cat's food and water, and filled an old oval dish with ripped-up newspapers for its litter tray. She placed teacups full of water for the cat on every empty surface in her room, and sometimes put small goldfish in them to keep him entertained.

The next-door neighbour loved to eat chocolates and biscuits. Angelica dug out the old tins from her rubbish bin and washed them. She went to a pharmacy and bought black liquorice menthol drops for sore throats, chocolates for constipation, pink nougat-looking chews for diarrhoea, sherbets for restlessness, pastilles that would make them drowsy, even stop their hearts if their hearts were weak.

She neatly arranged them in the tins. She stole some paper from the chemist's study and wrote LOVE, DADDY on them in a convincing imitation of his scrawl. She sent them to the children's boarding schools.

Angelica had once been a member of many societies. She was a suffragette and a socialist. Angelica had met her husband at a socialist union meeting; he had worked at a different factory then, but Angelica got him a job at hers. It was a place that produced what her husband called 'unnecessary, frivolous things'.

The factory was open all hours; sometimes they had night shifts and sometimes they had day shifts. When they both had a day shift, after work they would go for a hurried walk in the botanical gardens in the hour before it closed, the flowers and leaves curling themselves up in the dark. After, he would cook her eggs and potatoes on a hotplate in his rented room, which they ate sitting on his bed. He would scowl if she dropped any bit of egg or potato on his blankets.

Though he did not want to get married, they moved in together, and Angelica threw away most of her own possessions: the cup with a crack in it, the stockings with holes, the picture that had grown a beard of black mould in its frame. She did so furtively. She did not want him to think she was wasteful, but she did not want him to think she was a dirty slug either.

After their daughter Celeste was born, they begged their boss to let them have opposite schedules so that Celeste would never be left alone, but their boss said it was impossible.

They sometimes left Celeste with a neighbour but after the neighbour's little dog bit Celeste, Angelica's husband bought a large birdcage from a pet shop and told Angelica they could leave Celeste in it with a few dolls and a bottle of milk. Instead, Angelica found a nursery. It seemed to have too many children, and there were unpleasant paintings of dancing clowns and bears on the walls and dangerous-looking metallic toys shaped like ponies and castles, but it was all they could afford. Angelica's husband complained that Celeste smelled like liverwurst whenever they picked her up.

Angelica's husband did not believe in celebrating birthdays, Christmas or other holidays, as he said they were capitalist inventions. So it was on no special occasion that Angelica bought Celeste a pretty green velvet hat. She thought it would look lovely on her daughter. Celeste's hair fell out, and her scalp and eyeballs turned green before she died.

It was Angelica's love of consumption, of buying things, that killed Celeste, her husband said. He hit Angelica's face with his set of keys several times before putting them gently in her hand and saying goodbye.

Her husband went to live with a young woman named May who was the daughter of a famous communist and only wore brown, saggy dresses with little round metal spectacles exactly like her father's.

Angelica did all the shopping for the chemist's household, and was able on these trips to do a little shopping of her own.

Though things produced with Ambrosia Ltd's green dye were banned, they were still available in many second-hand and antique shops in great quantities as the public rushed to get rid of it all, and there was the occasional dusty shop whose proprietors hadn't read the newspapers and had failed to remove the products from their shelves.

These, Angelica hunted down. She wore a scarf around her face, and gloves to protect her hands.

She bought wallpaper (she measured the chemist's bedroom to make sure she had enough), extra-large women's dresses, green suits, hats, gloves, scarves, curtains, a green baby's pram, children's tin toys shaped like frogs, a set of clothbound green Ancient Greek books, six pairs of green shoes for ladies, men and children.

Though she saw a lot of alluring green furniture, it was always too heavy for her to carry. Instead, she bought rolls and rolls of fabric, with the intention to cover all the furniture in his bedroom. She bought empty, dusty absinthe bottles with poisonous green labels, a hand-painted green tea set, green taffeta ballet shoes, capes, ribbons, small pale green silk buttons, appliqués in the shapes of flowers, a green straw hat, a green backgammon set, plush green bears, pots of green paint she would use to paint his crocodile a vivid, horrid, shade. Now and then she felt blindly attracted by an object – a long green silk dress with a white ribbon around the waist, a faint green painting of a tree.

She put everything she bought in an unused room in the basement of the house, not far from her bedroom. When she walked by it, she felt it pulsating. She had dreams that all the green things merged into one huge creature: a toad, a dragon or a giant witch's head.

She had dreams she went into museums where all the paintings were in shades of green, or grocers' that only sold green food – wondrous big jellies, apples, mouldy cheese, jars of mint sauce and gherkins.

The chemist would never see the cook: Angelica would stab the cook in the kitchen and lock his body in his bedroom. She would cook the chemist's meals herself, but she didn't want to poison him that way.

The chemist would go into his bedroom and not notice all the changes until she had locked the door behind him. He would have nothing to wear, nothing to sit on or touch that wasn't poison, and soon he would know it.

A Novel (or Poem) About Fan, Aged 11 Years or The Zoo

'He feeds upon her face by day and night.'

CHRISTINA ROSSETTI

Jenny had been a painter's model for twenty years, ever since a filthy man with a golden beard and red mutton chops had stopped her on the street when she was a child selling flowers with her mother. Her mother made the man buy all their remaining flowers – cheap browning carnations, which were the last flowers they were ever to sell. The man said he was a painter and he liked Jenny's face.

Jenny's mother took off her daughter's hat and said, 'And look at those curls, sir.' Jenny's curls were dark brown.

By the time she was thirty-one years old, Jenny had had ten children, born not just from the artist with the golden beard and red mutton chops, but from various painters, sculptors and engravers in Britain. None of these artists had married her. She still lived with her mother. Jenny now found white hairs like loose bits from a broken spider's web on her head. She dyed her hair with used tea leaves to keep it chestnut.

After the fourth child she had started to name her children after objects she wanted but could not afford: Piano, Stove, Grand Fern. The children grew to resemble the objects they stood in for. Piano was a girl with a wide mouth and large, orderly teeth. She ate with her mouth open, grinned and talked all the time. She liked sweets, which turned a tooth or two black. Stove was a squat boy, with black hair, warm and temperamental; Grand Fern was thin and sickly green. Most cruelly, Jenny named a little boy Dog after she was unable to decide what kind of dog she wished for. The boy mainly liked to eat meat, which they could not afford often; he subsisted on beef bouillon and sometimes asked butchers for bones. Out of love, Jenny once stole a finger bone and a rib bone from an artist's anatomical skeleton, but they were made of plaster and crumbled in her bag before she could give them to him.

The children had a variety of hair colours and faces. Some of them had sat for artists already, as angels, shepherd boys, fairies and so forth, although not Fan, aged eleven, whose copper-coloured hair appealed to no artist.

Fan was the daughter of an engraver from Edinburgh. She had his face exactly, minus the moustache. Jenny no longer worked for him, after a bit of engraving acid fell onto her hands, creating a red spot she had to cover with paint. Unlike the hair of all the other children, Fan's orange hair was kept short as it was not worth the trouble of keeping long. It was not beautiful, Granny said.

All the other children, even the boys, had long hair in shades of gold, chestnut, ebony.

'If we are desperate,' said Granny, 'we can chop it and sell it for wigs and decorations.' This made the children weep, even the boys. Fan's cut hair was thrown into the chamber pot, or the fireplace.

The windows and floors and walls of their home – an attic three floors above a shop – were covered in Persian carpets to keep out the draughts. They were secondhand carpets, ones Granny had been given, or bought at a greatly reduced price, and they carried stains of wine and fine gravy and desserts none of them had ever eaten. There was a fireplace with green floral tiles in which they burned whatever they could and about which they huddled in cold weather.

One artist had left boxes and boxes of cheap spoons at their house, after discovering he'd got Jenny pregnant. They were not silver. His father had been a cutlery merchant and it was all he had to give. He was known to smear paint onto his canvases using forks, spoons and knives.

The children made dolls out of the spoons by wrapping cloth around their handles and sticking paper faces on them with horse glue. They tried to use them as mirrors, although they couldn't see anything reflected in them besides a pink blur like a bit of boiled pork or blancmange. They invented mysterious spoon games, hitting them against each other or against plates to make music.

They tried to sell them on the street, at markets, but people complained that they bent and broke or left a funny smell on food, and Jenny was afraid the man would discover they were selling them and demand them back. Granny put them in her hair as decorations, where they gathered dandruff, scabs and lice, which Granny spooned into the fireplace.

They received a letter from a new young painter. Granny had come across his work and thought his paintings very flat and muddy. He was younger than Jenny, and a friend of a painter they knew named Brown who was violent, but the letter from the new painter was on fine, perfumed and decorated paper. He wanted Jenny to pose as an Arthurian witch, he wrote: Morgan le Fay.

Granny went with Jenny and three of the prettiest children to see his studio.

His studio was a large greenhouse in the back garden of a house which they supposed him to live in, though it was empty and cold when they walked through.

The floor of the greenhouse was covered with old letters, newspapers, Persian carpets and small tattered wool blankets, all held together with animal shit, pee, paint and fruit rinds and cores: oranges and lemons, pomegranates, grapes, and even bits of pineapple – Granny recognised the smell for she had tried pineapple once – rotting into the strangely mapped floor.

There were many animals chirping and lulling around, ones they couldn't name: small brown bear-like creatures, tiny green dragons, colourful birds with large beaks, a creature with grey, black and white fur and very human little hands, and snakes the yellow colour of a dying person. There were also creatures they could name: repulsive small dogs with sunken-in, dirty faces, monkeys, an armadillo, and a white exotic-looking cow who lived in the garden, eating flowers.

There wasn't a fireplace, but a black woodstove, like one from a fairy tale with bowlegged limbs. There was a pot on top of this stove that smelled of beef. There were vases filled with feathers instead of flowers, from peacocks, magpies, white ones from a bird they couldn't name. And there were many plants – basil pots, orange and lemon trees – which the children reached for, smelling.

The painter said he loved the smell of basil. There was once, he told them, a woman who hid a man's head in a pot of basil.

The painter, who had long golden hair and was very thin, had appeared from behind a potted palm tree. He didn't wear a suit, but instead a long beige frock with a brown coat over the top, and a dirty piece of purple silk wound many times round his neck. His father was supposed to be Italian, but Granny thought he looked too pale to be Italian, and when she told him he laughed and asked if she'd ever seen a painting by Botticelli.

The painter was notorious for having had a painter wife – who'd died, so Granny had heard. He had some of her drawings in the studio, pale pastel things, now stuck together with bird shit. Wanting to be an artist like her husband had been the death of her, said Granny. Jenny had heard from another artist that a collector had tried to buy them, but the painter wouldn't sell them. He had emptied the house in which he and his wife had lived and moved into the greenhouse, into the wild forest he had created.

'We have many children too, with the looks of Jenny, if you are needing angels, fairies, imps and beggar children,' said Granny, pushing the three most beautiful she'd brought with them forward.

The artist painted Jenny wearing a grey cloak and looking sinister, surrounded by ivy, and again in a brocade gown looking out of a window in the empty house. He painted her, deathly looking, with one of her children posed asleep or dead on her lap.

The children began to call his studio the zoo.

'When are we going to the zoo next?'

'It smells at the zoo.'

'Why can't I go to the zoo?'

They had never been to a real zoo. After being in

the painter's studio, a real zoo, with animals in cages and labels describing what they were, would have been disappointing. At the studio, they could see a mysterious long-snouted brown thing under a chair, a colourful bird sitting on top of a lampshade, a snake, the colour of a rosy cheek, curled around an umbrella. A strange sound from the cupboard, a monkey warming itself by the fireplace, the small cold chain round his neck attached to nothing, dragging behind him like a second tail. Biting, scratching death.

One of Jenny's pretty little boys became obsessed with picking things off the floor with a stick, believing he would find a coin or some other treasure on the greenhouse floor. He often picked up orange peels, put them in his pocket and chewed on them later, or held them against the stove till they burned and smelled nice.

He ate a smear of white paint after poking it with his stick to test the consistency.

'I thought it were cream that felled on the floor,' he said weakly, when he told them he felt sick after.

The painter forced his fingers down the boy's throat and made him vomit, then gave him tea and candied ginger and said if he wasted his paint again he would feed him to the snake.

The painter invited Jenny, Granny and all the children over for a dinner. He had changed into a black suit whose sleeves and legs were spotted with mud. The dinner was held in the cold house, in a green-papered room. A table and chairs had been put out, and the fire lit, but the floor was still covered with dust and there weren't any pictures or prints on the walls. They were served roast meat, jelly, mulligatawny soup and lobster.

Granny and Jenny brought Fan with them because they were worried she would destroy their home if they left her alone.

Over dinner Fan said she disliked jellies, for they looked like glass, and glass was very sharp. She couldn't be convinced that the jellies were soft, even when the painter delved into them with a spoon and said it was thicker but softer than water.

She also didn't want the painter to take apart the lobster. She asked if she could have it, but he laughed and said it was for eating, but that he would buy her a new, fresh one – there were many lobsters to be had.

After he'd divided up the flesh, Fan took the pieces of shell from everyone's plate and put them in her small, ragged handbag – a stinking rotting puzzle she would put together then take apart again.

The painter said Fan was the most beautiful and interesting creature he had ever seen, and he would like to paint her.

*

The first time she went over to model, he showed her that he'd bought another lobster, a live one, and was keeping it for her in a large porcelain tureen. He'd named it Mr Lobster. They fed it worms, bits of meat and eel, but he said a lobster would eat another lobster if it had the chance, and would eat her too. 'Why are you so fond of something so hideous and so cruel?' he asked.

'It's not hideous,' replied Fan. 'It wears red armour and has whiskers and lives in the sea, which is a very beautiful place.'

He posed Fan in gold gauze wings and a bronze silk dress, holding the yellow snake. She wasn't afraid of it. She liked the furless animals most, the ones with scales and shells. He posed her as Joan of Arc, the Christ child, a young Virgin Mary, a shepherd's daughter, a Renaissance musician.

'I don't know how to play the lute, so I feel like a fool holding it,' said Fan. 'I am a novelist and poet, and so should like to hold a pen. My novels will take place in the ocean. *In* the ocean, not on it.'

'Keep still,' said the painter.

He took the entire family for a picnic in the largest park in the city. He wore a long black cape over his suit and carried a woven basket full of food and nice china, some of which the children broke. Jenny, Granny and all the children looked tattered in the sunlight – crumpled paper flowers on their dirty hats. The painter did too, with paint and animal hairs on his cape, his golden hair blown about by the wind, exposing bald patches. Something made all the children sick – maybe the meat pies, or the fresh fruit, or the boiled eggs, or the minced crab, which Fan petted and cooed over before she ate. Jenny was very ashamed and took them all home as they whined and held their bottoms.

The chamber pot was soon all dirty and used. As only one at a time could go, they had to use the teapots and the teacups – everything was soon filled, a ghastly tea party, and when it was dark Granny took each bit of crockery out one by one and threw the contents into the street and said to herself, 'I hope it rains before morning, I do hope it rains before morning.'

The painter put Fan into a white nightie, but it was too long for her and it lay around her feet like spilled cream. He made her stand in a large glass punch bowl, holding the nightie up, to paint her feet standing in water. The water wasn't warmed, as he worried the glass would shatter.

On her next visit, he filled a metal tub with hot water and told her to get in, again wearing the nightie. He put real lilies and weeds he had taken from a pond in with her.

When she said it was getting cold, he poured more water from a hot kettle into it, but sometimes he didn't listen when she said, 'I'm cold,' and just kept on painting. He wanted her to look a bit blue around the lips.

'Pretend you're Mr Lobster. No, don't move your hands about like that, pretend you're Mr Lobster in your mind. Stay still. You're dying, a dying maiden.'

In the corner of the painting there was to be a swimming water rat. The painter had bought a live one for the purpose, but as he could not keep it still, as still as Fan could be under his direction, he killed it and arranged its corpse in the position he liked.

Jenny's eldest daughter, Jane, was already dead. At fifteen, she'd been sent to model for a sculptor. After the second session, she'd cried and said her stomach hurt and that the sculptor had stuck his arm inside her. She was bleeding. Granny wrapped her in hot towels and called her a whore.

When she gave birth it was very small and died. 'Good,' said Granny. 'The sculptor was monstrous-looking; the child would've been ugly.'

'Throw it in the chamber pot,' said Granny, but Jane threw a rotten potato wrapped in a cloth in it instead, and kept the baby bundled in handkerchiefs under her pillow. It smelled for a bit, then dried up.

The other children knew about it, but didn't quite understand where it came from; they felt it was a toy that belonged only to Jane and, though they took it out from under her pillow and examined it when she wasn't there, they didn't play with it as they did each other's toys.

When Jane died they made sure to hide it under her frock so she could be buried with it.

When the painter was finished painting Fan in the tub for the day, he let her sit by the woodstove, with the armadillo, whose skin she liked, on her lap. He toasted muffins for them, and gave her red wine to return the colour to her cheeks. He read to her, as she didn't know how to read or write, though he promised he would teach her eventually. She dictated her stories out loud to him, and he wrote them on nice paper with blue pen, and let her look at what he had written down after.

'It looks like a drawing of the sea. Have you written down my story or have you just drawed the sea?'

When Fan became deathly ill, the painter no longer allowed her in the studio, though Granny gently suggested Fan move in there; he could paint her dying, to soak the last bit of colour out of used tea leaves. He sent a wooden box full of oranges for her. She ate one and threw it up, the pieces chewed and acrid.

He put her stories and the sketches he'd done of her in a folio in her coffin, covered her face, and asked Granny to snip him a piece of her orange hair, which he smelled then put in his pocket. Four months after Fan died, the painter returned to her grave and had her coffin dug up so that he could retrieve his drawings. He was going to leave her poems and novels inside, but the friend who helped him dig up the coffin suggested they publish them, that perhaps they were interesting, though written by a child, but neither had the money then to have them printed and bound. Still, they took them. If one had ever seen the ground under an apple tree in late autumn, when picking has been neglected and the apples are strewn about decomposing, nibbled here and there, sinking into the ground, insects burrowing through, they would know how the child looked in her coffin, though here there was also a tattered bit of cloth that had once been Fan's dress.

The painter put the drawings of Fan in an exhibition in the house, which still stood empty, along with the paintings of her, and many were sold. Fan's stories were lost in the general muck of his studio.

'She was a beautiful one after all,' said Granny. 'Many people think it, don't they?'

Mr Elephant

In Margate—

There are many antique shops, that's why I moved here; not for the sea, which a few have said would be good for my health.

Crockery, crockery! Pots, cups, vases, plates.

I live in a hotel with low ceilings and carpeted floors that faces the sea directly. The sea is a noisome neighbour, it crumples tissues and snores and smells of sardines, but I just need to hold a cutlet or chops out of the window to have them salted. I keep crockery all along the walls of every room, white and blue only, like misshapen or flattened globes. I keep all my things in crockery: tea in a china jar marked 'Tea', needles in a cream jug, a roll of toilet paper in a teapot on top of the toilet, a soup tureen full of socks! My makeup in sugar bowls – violet, yellow, green, blue, depending on my mood, like one of those rings one buys at fairs.

All the crockery chatters like teeth when I walk and dance about, too; when those above or below do, my rooms become the building's mouth.

I like the noise; it competes with the noise of the sea.

The sea collects crockery too, we have that in common, but she crunches it up like saltine crackers then animates the little bits. I have a pot of horse glue for putting mine back together when they crack.

I don't like fish, tentacles, molluscs, seaweed; I like sausages, liver, chops, marrow and cutlets. I don't like jelly – particularly with things floating in it, like a stilled chunk of sea. Once, I thought of filling the sea with gelatin powder to stop its constant noise, to hire ships filled with gelatin powder – there would be enough gelatin powder packets, enough pigs in the world, I think.

I like meat and tea.

For example:

Chops, tea,

Liver, tea

Marrowbone, tea.

&c

Sometimes I make a cup of broth or tea and having forgotten which it is, do not know until I taste it.

There are many butcher shops in Margate, too: the antique and butcher shops keep me well. I have to go out for more crockery as often as I have to for meat.

I can't explain why I like blue and white crockery, but brown food.

The carpets don't match the crockery; the carpets are cream and pink like flattened squares of raw meat.

Twice a week a woman comes to give me ballroom dancing lessons. She wears a wig that wiggles slightly as we dance. Interestingly, she is not bald underneath, but has very fine blonde hair. I suppose she hides it because such hair attracts seedy men, but her wig has a false smell I find unpleasant, like a plastic bowl. I found a well-preserved grey wig at an antique shop, made out of natural materials – human or mohair – but she was offended at the suggestion she wear it, and it now sits in one of my teapots. Once, I said to her, 'Lance my cyst, will you,' handing her a sewing needle that I had heated on the stove.

She would not oblige, and I understood.

The smell of my burst cysts was intolerable, like sour, dirty feet, like something desperately spoiled.

They were on my fingers, neck, torso and buttocks. I wanted her to lance the large one on my neck which was planted uncomfortably close to my Adam's apple. I did it myself, looking in the bathroom mirror. The mirror I had was too filthy, so I put a new mirror in front of it, one on top of the other. The oldest one hangs, I haven't seen it for ages, and there are two others perched on the sink. I don't want to throw away or irritate any mirrors for what they have seen and absorbed, but the surface of them is cracked and covered in soap suds and the soft-boiled-egg-like excretions from my cysts. The mirrors aren't as troublesome or as mysterious as the grandfather clock.

The grandfather clock—

Teeth—

I have opened the grandfather clock up and there are no teeth to be found, but they arrive on the hour, when it chimes, all on the floor around and underneath the clock's legs – like a bloodless mouth has been hit inside, for the teeth are always dry like museum pieces. Once, just once, there was a long, slightly curved tooth among the human ones, which resembled a small rhinoceros horn.

Along the corners of wood, along the gears of the clock, there are no teeth – I've looked, I've examined it all like a dentist would, yet still they arrive on the hour. I inherited the grandfather clock from an aunt and it's very old – from when grandfather clocks were first made, I believe; one of the first.

I put all the teeth in vases – I have filled three now, they come in such abundance. They have a very mild odour, and when it becomes too much I'll empty the vases into the sea.

Crockery, crockery!

Avalon

I once had a job in a basement sauna in an expensive part of town. You had to walk down a flight of steps towards a green façade which said 'AVALON SAUNA'. The one window had old newspapers glued to it, bars and curtains, but you could see a dim purplish light behind it.

Before, I had worked in an antiquarian bookshop nearby. I was fired because the owner kept asking me out for dinner and I kept saying no as his breath smelled and he had beady eyes that were always staring at me and my female co-workers.

He would corner us between shelves and recite Rabbie Burns poems ('Wee, sleekit, cowrin, tim'rous beastie,' he would say, adjusting his corduroy trousers), which I hated – all the employees hated Rabbie Burns because the owner loved him so much. There was even a lithograph of Burns hanging in the bookshop, and I cursed his side-burns every day. He accused me of stealing a first edition of *The Golden Bough* out of spite, though I saw him take the edition home himself in his coat pocket.

The sauna was owned by a couple named the Van Der Bijls.

They owned the whole building, so the tenants on the floors above could not complain about the damp from the sauna, or the seedy clientele who loitered around on the street in front, smoking and sometimes vomiting, always smelling of sweat.

Because of the damp, the Van Der Bijls did not live in the building, but in one around the corner. Either Mr or Mrs Van Der Bijl worked the reception counter, taking the payments for the sauna treatments and giving out keys for the locker room where customers put their coats, hats, umbrellas and briefcases.

The front door of the sauna was always locked from the inside. There was a buzzer customers had to ring, then the door opened into a claustrophobic reception room with a teller's desk behind glass, thick red carpet and a Chinese vase full of fake flowers and branches, covered in white fairy lights, half of which did not work anymore. On the wall behind the teller counter was a very old-looking Union Jack flag. To the left of the teller desk was a metal padded door, which led into the locker room and then the saunas.

It was like one very large bathroom inside in the sauna, all tiled. Few of the tiles matched; the Van Der Bijls had bought them from various bathroom shops on discount, or pilfered them from abandoned houses. Some were really beautiful, with art nouveau designs of flowers and butterflies, and others had ducks or skeletons on them. There was one I really liked of a skull wearing a sombrero that I vowed to steal.

The sauna was not properly ventilated, it was just a basement with tiles and showers and steam, so the tiles were constantly falling off the walls. We had a pot of horse glue to stick the tiles back on when they fell off – one of our many chores.

There were wooden stools and various fainting chairs covered in green linoleum for men to lie on, a few miserable potted palms, all yellow from too much water and no sunlight.

I was put on my first shift with a girl named Nell. She had red frizzy hair, a tattoo of a purple flower on one arm, and lots of bruises which I saw when she changed into our work uniforms.

The Van Der Bijls made us wear white lab coats, which became hot and sweaty in the sauna, so we wore nothing underneath.

I had no idea what I needed to do on my first shift, but Nell taught me.

I didn't know how to give a massage, but Nell said all you needed to do was hit and punch their back as if you hated them while they lay on their stomachs on the fainting chairs, or stood under one of the showers.

They also liked to have a smaller towel rubbed between their butt cheeks, 'which were always dirty and sore,' Nell said, so it had to be done gently.

'For the front,' she said, 'you rub it up and down until it's emptied, then it is clean.'

I told her it sounded an awful lot like a hand job and she told me not to repeat that to the Van Der Bijls.

She told me which men not to touch: either they didn't like to be, or they only came to touch other men. This, Nell taught me to turn a blind eye to, saying, 'Poor souls, nowhere else to go, except for the graveyards and they are cold and muddy,' and told me not to stare at the details or particularities of each body after seeing me eye a wooden leg (I wondered if it would rot, coming to the sauna so often, and I believe it did, because one day he came in with a new leg, made out of dark red plastic) and various sores, enlargements, discoloured abnormalities. I saw a man with testicles the size of my head, and a man with a tapeworm wiggling out of his anus – hungry and seeking food. One man brought a tin of lemon-yellow cream, which smelled terrible, and made us rub it on his dry butt cheeks, though the other customers complained about the scent. Nell whispered to me that the cream was meant for a baby's rashes. There was a man with a large open wound on his thigh, which looked more crusty and rotted and disgusting every time he came to the sauna. We found a live snake sliding around the floors. Nell stepped on it with one foot, but it escaped and disappeared down a drain before she could fully kill it.

When there were few guests or none, we had to hose down the floors and pick up all the dropped dirty towels. One of us took them in a giant sack to a laundry down the street, and brought the bill to Mr or Mrs Van Der Bijl.

We had mops to clean up faeces, cigarette butts, hair and whatever else was left on the floors and fainting chairs. I found teeth, toe- and fingernails, signet rings, ballpoint pens.

Mr Van Der Bijl cleaned out the locker room himself because there was always leftover change, small bottles of gin, cigarettes and nice ties left there. Once someone left a very old painting of some dead pigeons and artfully arranged apricots which the Van Der Bijls took home, saying the owner wouldn't want it anyway because it had become ruined from the sauna steam.

My first few shifts I brought a book to read during the slow hours but it became all damp and the pages stuck together and Mr Van Der Bijl yelled at me for reading.

Two doors down from the sauna was a corner shop that sold lots of bad, wilted-looking fruit – caved-in oranges, wrinkly apples and slimy slices of pineapple. Nell always bought it all and said it was much healthier than fruit that came in jars filled with syrup which ruined one's teeth – a girl she used to work with always ate figs, peaches and pineapples in syrup then her teeth all fell out and she couldn't afford dentures and tried to glue white mint candies to her gums with the sauna's pot of horse glue and she ended up having to get her stomach pumped as she swallowed too much of it. We made below minimum wage because certain parts of the job were not within the law. It was less than I had made at the bookshop.

In the entrance of a sauna was a porcelain pot for tips, which was shaped like a lamb on a stool. It was always filled but the Van Der Bijls took all the tips for themselves. The reason our lab coats had no pockets and we weren't allowed stockings was so we couldn't hide any of the tips on our bodies. 'I used to stick the coins up my vagina,' said Nell, 'but then I got a weird infection and my pee turned green. It wasn't worth it – it was mostly coppers anyway.'

The girl I had replaced had died from an abortion she gave herself. A doctor gave her a package of tools and pills and told her to do it herself at home, but she didn't follow the instructions properly and she bled to death. 'It's funny,' said Nell, 'she used to always work on shift with a bald kewpie doll stuffed between her breasts, which she called Baby Harold.

'I don't sit anywhere in here while on shift,' Nell said. 'I can't take birth control because it makes me feel sick and I have a fear of getting pregnant from all the drops of sperm here.'

I followed her advice, though my legs got tired on shift.

We both peed standing up, straight into drains when no men were around.

The sauna was open twenty-four hours a day, and girls were on rotating shifts. Sometimes Nell and I were put on in the daytime, and sometimes we had to work the whole night, but always together.

Mr Van Der Bijl and Mrs Van Der Bijl only really saw each other when changing shifts. They kissed each other dryly, handed each other schnitzels wrapped in tinfoil and discussed the business. They loved money more than they loved each other.

The worst customers were the rugby players, who were full of veins and muscles and sweated everywhere. They didn't like to be touched – their bodies were their bread and butter – so they just slapped each other with towels and laughed and showered and left a gigantic mess of bandages and hairs. One of them, as a joke, always left a giant shit, as big as a brown mink stole, somewhere on the floor for us to clean.

Solemn red-faced men came at night. They were always the dirtiest; perhaps the sauna was the only time they came into contact with water.

Once I saw the bookshop owner, but I hid behind a fainting chair and made Nell clean him. A few old men refused to take off their wool caps and bowler hats and these became damp and smelly. I imagined they had thin wispy hair and scabs that they were ashamed of or skinless caps of withered skull. A lot of their clothes smelled, too – oily tweeds and cashmere scarves, which they just put back on again, which made our work feel pointless.

One of those men always brought a dirty bookshop tote bag inside with him, though he was otherwise naked. Thinking it must contain something precious he was afraid of having stolen in the locker room, I looked inside as it hung from his shoulder as I was cleaning his buttocks. The tote bag was full of pebbles, sticks and squashed pears. The man had a dreamy look in his eyes and always drooled.

There was a man whose almost hairless torso I admired. He just came in to shower. I longed to clean and hit his body. Nell said she used to admire him too but got bored of it.

I made my first big mistake with an elderly man.

'Careful, I have a haemorrhoid there,' he said, as I crouched down with a towel in front of his buttocks.

I rubbed the towel back and forth as carefully as I could but at one point he howled and turned around, punching me in the face. I fell down on the tiles; I could feel one cracking under my spine and my nose was bleeding. He made Nell, who went to help me up, finish the job. His breasts were red and shaking with anger. My lab coat was covered in blood from my nose and the Van Der Bijls made me pay for the laundry bill. Because my face looked disgusting, I was given a week off work, unpaid. I ate frugally, grapes I got on discount, toast and cans of soup, and went to museums, a big plaid scarf wrapped round the bottom half of my face to cover the bruises. I never saw the special exhibitions because those cost money, only the same things over and over again: the same vases, stones and statues in the permanent collections.

I saw the man who had punched me, wearing red trousers and a hunting coat, going into an expensive house near the museum, holding the hand of a little girl in a fur coat, but he did not recognise me.

Nell invited me over for dinner on her day off. I had a half-full bottle of crème de menthe. I poured it into an old perfume vial, which it filled, and it looked quite glamorous. I brought it to drink.

She lived alone in a furnished attic, which had far too much furniture in it. This explained why Nell was covered in bruises: she bumped into all the edges all the time. Most of the drawers and wardrobes had padlocks on them because they were full of the landlord's things.

'There were too many men to clean without you,' she said. 'It was exhausting.'

She made us aspic from a packet of powder, saying, 'It's good for your bones.' It was her favourite thing to eat along with fresh fruit.

'I would love to work in a tea or coffee shop. They always close at 6 p.m. so you always know when you're going to bed, and you can take home the leftover pastries that don't sell,' said Nell dreamily. We were both drowsy and drunk from the crème de menthe.

She told me things that could not be said in the sauna.

'The Van Der Bijls rented a room in one of the flats they own above the sauna to a girl who worked there, though her sauna salary wasn't enough to pay rent and eat, which they well knew but they didn't lower the price. I once saw her eating something that had fallen on the floor of the locker room, from one of the customers. The mattress in her rented bedroom was covered in black mould, and so were the curtains and even the lampshade; she was coughing all the time. The Van Der Bijls made a big deal out of her cough and said they would pay for her to stay in a sanatorium. She must have died there,' said Nell, 'because she never returned to the sauna.'

Once a year the Van Der Bijls went on holiday to South Africa and left their cousin Geert in charge of the sauna; Geert had a blond toupee and always raped one of the girls.

The idea of Geert disgusted me so much, I felt I would be raped next, that I threw up all the crème de menthe and aspic in Nell's bathroom sink. My vomit looked like cheap-coloured washing-up liquid.

Nell said we ought to get our revenge on them before their holiday and I agreed.

Since Nell had worked at the sauna the longest, the Van Der Bijls had taught her to fix the pipes when there were leaks. She would undo all the work she had done over the years with a wrench. We chose a time when the Van Der Bijls switched shifts, going over accounts together in the office, to drown them.

We stuffed package after package of steel wool down all the drains and turned on all the taps and showers.

Nell told the Van Der Bijls there was a leak in the back of the sauna while I waited outside. She ran out while they inspected it and bolted the door with a lock and chain we'd bought from a hardware shop and put a decorative concrete statue of a woman we stole from a nearby private garden in front of the door. I remembered that the man with the beautiful torso was one of the customers in there and I thought of breaking through the window and carrying him out safe in my arms, but it was too late, it would ruin everything. We left. I thought I heard shouting inside. There was no back fire exit.

Nell said we might as well go to the Van Der Bijls' home address and see what we could steal as they would never go there again.

It was a four-storey stone townhouse with thick red curtains on all the windows. Nell opened the front door with the keys she'd stolen from the sauna office. It led into a foyer with a grand staircase and a large main floor door that was locked. The staircase was covered in broken glass. I was just wearing ballet flats so Nell piggybacked me up the stairs in her Doc Martens.

There was thick red carpet everywhere on the next floor, even in the hall, bathroom and kitchen – the same red carpet as in the sauna reception room.

We looked in the fridge. We found pâté, green grapes, milk, an open tin of custard that had gone off (Nell tried it with a spoon), roast beef wrapped in tinfoil, prune juice in a glass jug, half a Brie and a cardboard container of duck eggs. There was a bottle of brandy on the counter, which we both drank from, carrying it around as we explored.

We found the painting the Van Der Bijls had stolen from the sauna in the bathroom, where it had been further ruined by condensation. There were dozens of other paintings on the walls, of women and partridges, Scottish landscapes, all cracked like old Easter eggs. There was a large knife and a dried ball of shit in the bathroom sink. The toilet had a fuzzy cloth covering. We both wanted to take a bath as neither of us had bathtubs in our apartments but the blue bathtub was dirty, with brown and grey streaks all over it, and caked around the edges with bars of expensive soap still in their paper wrapping, patterned like wallpaper and water-stained.

There was an unfinished game of draughts on one of the tables in the living room, and hard-looking cushions on all the furniture, with floral or Union Jack patterns. There was more art, family photographs – Nell pointed out Geert. Nell picked up one of the cushions off the couch in the living room. The underside of the cushion was covered in tiny white worms.

She threw it back down. We didn't take anything. She threw the rest of the brandy bottle on the floor where it smashed, as we were afraid there were tiny worms in it too.

On some house steps a few doors down, I held Nell as she was sick. The sight of her vomiting made me feel nauseated too, and soon I was throwing up the brandy, a puddle forming by our feet, but I felt no matter how much we were sick we could never be clean inside again. I imagined tiny versions of the Van Der Bijls in my stomach, floating, dead, in spit, and I retched again.

The Poison Garden

The Margate city council in charge of the Tudor House Museum didn't hire Lil because of her art history degree. They hired her for her long red hair, which they thought would look splendid draped across the shoulders of an Elizabethan-style dress. Her face, though young, was long and crooked, but women of the Tudor era weren't beautiful either by birth or design. It was a Tudor house museum with nothing Tudor left inside. It had been lived in until the 1970s, after which layer upon layer of life was stripped away by the Margate Heritage Council – wallpaper, carpet, a cast-iron Victorian stove, insulation, iron pipes, the bare worm-eaten wood of the Tudor era exposed. They nailed a picture of Queen Elizabeth I to one of the chimneys, framed and varnished to look like a painting. A plaster feast of Tudor foods was made by a group of local women: a pig's head, apples, loaves and a roast chicken. Lil, living Lil, would give it more authenticity.

Margate was a seaside town known for white nineteenth-century hotels where sick people once stayed, and flashy amusements. The Tudor House looked out of place; many people who passed by assumed it was an abandoned Alpine restaurant.

On her first day, a few weeks after the interview, Lil showed up with her hair chopped off, wearing earrings shaped like seahorses and large plastic glasses. She had a tartan suitcase which she put in the ticket booth, saying she had just arrived on the train from London and would drop it off at her flat later. In her suitcase was a sleeping bag, an electric kettle, a pot, a jar of unbranded instant coffee, clothes and a stack of books she had forgotten to return to the Courtauld library.

Lil was given a set of keys and put in charge of everything. Everyone else who worked in the museum was a volunteer, under her charge.

At a few local charity shops, using money from the entrance tickets, Lil bought two hard, thin chairs with velvet seats, a large red embroidered blanket that looked vaguely like a tapestry and a reproduction of Hans Sloane's nautilus shell, a scene of sixteenth-century Dutch battles etched onto its sides, the inner coil carved to look like a helmet, only visible as one from the front, which she put on display with an information card at the museum. She bolted it to a table, but didn't put glass over it, telling the museum council that visitors loved objects they could

86

interact with. Most of the volunteers disliked how male visitors would stick their fingers in the shell, but they didn't say anything to Lil or each other. She didn't wear any of the Elizabethan costumes they had, but hung them on a clothing rack and put a mirror in a corner where visitors could put them on and photograph themselves.

Lil discovered there were mice living in the plaster feast, but left them to their business, sweeping away their droppings each morning, hiding them as she hid herself. She didn't have a flat of her own, and the museum wage wasn't enough for one. She slept on the second floor of the Tudor House, beside one of the giant fireplaces, which were no longer in use. There wasn't a shower or bathtub in the house anymore, only a toilet open to visitors with a large bottle of antibacterial soap and a paper-towel dispenser. Lil ran the tap hot, stuck one end of a towel with the soap lathered on it underneath, and washed herself with it.

One of the cupboards was stacked full of metal children's chairs, and old Halloween costumes which at night created a nest to throw her sleeping bag on.

The Tudor House was surrounded by a garden that did not contain much: some small trees, a palm, pansies and purple hyacinths. Lil ordered new seeds through a Wiccan shop in London and from various questionable websites. Queen Anne's lace, juniper, hemlock, rue, belladonna or deadly nightshade. Pennyroyal, nutmeg, laurel.

When it was ready, she charged visitors £3 to view her poison garden, £5 total for the house and garden tour. Numbers increased significantly. The city council approved, and sent a letter to Lil that would not arrive for several weeks, telling her that she was doing splendidly.

She handwrote warning signs to not *smell, eat or touch the plants!* And provided explanations of the harm each could do. Seizures, dizziness, fainting, abortion, death.

'This garden is a woman's friend,' she said to one of the Tudor House's elderly volunteers, who didn't laugh.

She installed a small fountain, demonic-looking water spilling from a griffin's mouth, made out of plastic imitating stone. She had written her master's thesis on fountains and was full of fascinating information on them that nobody wanted to hear.

There was only a small fence around her garden, so short a toddler could step over it. It was historically authentic but it wasn't secure. People trampled in at night on drunken dares, or to make dangerous love among the plants, or to steal clippings for use. She turned on her torch upstairs, put on one of her costume police helmets and pretended to be a security guard when they did, but couldn't tell the museum board because they didn't know she was living there.

The young man never tried to sneak in at night, only during opening hours, believing he blended in with the tourists. He paid the entrance fee. He was tall with bad posture, a large nose, dark, neatly cut hair and dark-framed glasses.

He smoked, which made others move away from him. He carried a *London Review of Books* tote bag, the bottom of it speckled with black ink from a leaky pen, so that from a distance it looked as though it had been dipped in bird shit. He studied the signs. He grabbed leaves and berries, stuffing them in his coat pocket. The first time, he had bare hands. After that, he wore black wool gloves.

He kept coming back. Either the plants weren't working and he was trying new ones, or it wasn't himself he was trying to kill.

Tom stood outside the Turner Contemporary Art Gallery. His wife, Esme, was inside looking at photographs. He had wanted to go outside for a minute, have a cigarette. There was a beggar sitting on the gallery steps who kept saying, 'I've just come from London . . .'

Esme had the type of face men like best: far-apart eyes, a small nose, a wide mouth – a face like another face that has been squished and stretched under a spatula or the palm of a hand, or a face that has retained the measure-ments and purity of a baby's, that hasn't grown outwards and increased in complexities and detail, only width-wise like a thick liquid being poured on a flat surface. Her hair was blonde, dyed a lighter shade of blonde than the blonde it was naturally, and she wore small hoop earrings and a white coat.

Tom dreaded the moment he would have to see the back of her coat, the blooming red stain he knew he'd find. Thank god they had already eaten lunch, at a trendy coffee place. He could take her straight home.

When he went back inside the gallery he stood behind her, obscuring the back of the coat from view. He said we'd best get home, and when she fell into step with him he held back a little, to look into a shop window, or grab another cigarette.

They were renting the middle flat in a large white terraced house and had only recently moved. Renting was a lie. It was an Airbnb. They were taking a short leave from London, where Tom worked in a bank and was also a poet. He didn't know if he would be much of a poet in Margate, but wandering around small side streets on his own carrying various things in his *London Review of Books* tote bag, peering past thin patterned curtains like flakes of tattooed skin, observing how the shopfront frames and white blinds of a denture shop looked like rows of teeth, he felt more like a poet than he did eating in good cafés and browsing in retro interior shops with his wife. He had said to Esme, 'I like Margate, it's charming and seedy in a way no part of London is anymore.'

There weren't any good bookshops in Margate, no blue commemorative plaques denoting those who had come and written before him.

Esme had wanted to be an actress or a model, but there were too many women who looked like her. She had a degree from Goldsmiths University and had had various jobs gained through her connections – at the BBC, at a magazine shop, as the nanny of a well-known artist's children.

She documented their stay in Margate on Instagram. The sun setting on the beach, plates of pleasing, colourful food, the bay window of the Airbnb, piles of the books Tom was reading, and excerpts from Tom's already published poems.

Tom also had an Instagram account. He posted two photos: the first a mannequin head in a shop window, the second a silver fork mysteriously left on the pavement, then decided that would be all. He used a sepia picture of Rilke for his profile.

Esme appreciated that he'd started cooking so much since they'd arrived in Margate: it made her feel more secure when she called him her partner instead of husband. They were a team.

It was lucky that in the kind of food she liked – vegetable 'bowls', Asian soups, salads – the abortifacients he was secretly feeding her were easy to hide. There would be no disguising them on chips or pizza. He tolerated their side effects with fortitude. Diarrhoea, stomach aches, sweaty hands and forehead, ailments that came across as part of his anxiety, the reason they'd come to Margate. To rest his nerves. She didn't tell him if she felt the same effects, would never say if she had diarrhoea to anyone. He ate whole bags of crisps by himself, standing in beach shelters and small squares, and splashed his face with cold seawater, crouching on the beach.

The first miscarriage was very early on; she had gone to the hospital and they had merely told her she couldn't handle her own periods, and to take some paracetamol.

The stain on her coat was the second, he knew. He filled her a hot-water bottle, purchased her some Green and Black's dark chocolate, took her white coat to a dry cleaner's. Things a supportive partner would do. Her used tampons were always very carefully wrapped in tissue paper before being thrown in the bin, so he would never see them, but once when she wasn't home, he had dug through the bin and unwrapped one. Only the top half was stained with blood, like a tiny ice lolly.

She hadn't seen a fertility expert yet, but she had downloaded a fertility app on her phone. She was only twenty-nine. He didn't want a child. Sure, if they had a child it would have the nicest, most expensive things. Both his and Esme's parents were well off. Tom had a good salary.

There was an antique shop in Margate with a basement room where everything was marked down to £1 because it was broken, or half missing, or not working. Chipped crockery, figurines with holes in them like nibbled-on chocolate Easter rabbits, single mittens and shoes, clothes with stains and moth holes, scratched records, old cameras for which film was no longer made. He had the sense that something awful was lurking underneath the piles – a piece of rotting food, a toy covered in brown smears, a dead animal, a large spider, some glistening terrible thing that he would find almost overwhelmingly aesthetically pleasing.

His child would never play or wear anything from that room, or even enter it.

He pretended that his position at the bank was lowlier than it was, that his degree from Harvard hadn't been necessary to get it, that he needed to work for a living. He had camouflaged himself so well that left-leaning people in the literary world wouldn't criticise him any more than they would someone who worked on the checkout at Tesco or McDonald's. He could be derisive of those who claimed to live in London off a few reviews a month, each paying no more than a hundred pounds.

Not long after they had arrived in Margate, he went through Esme's makeup bag in the bathroom. He took a green eyeshadow – he had never seen her wear it – and stuck one of his fingers in it. He smeared it on his face until there was none left in the compact, and he looked like a bogeyman, his face a sickly green. He added blue eyeshadow to his eyes and chin.

When he heard her come through the main door, he hurriedly washed it off with a wet towel, even though he had already locked the bathroom door.

On her CV, Lil put 'Director, Tudor House Museum, Margate'.

Her favourite meal was chips and a pickled egg from a famous fish and chip shop on the promenade. She would mush the egg on top of the chips and add large squeezes of various sauces, white, brown, red, but she mostly made do with bananas, chocolate bars, cream crackers that were on discount because they were crumbly and the way 'CREAM CRACKERS' was written on them had accidentally turned out creepy, and tins of kidney beans which tasted like soft pebbles.

If the young man was suicidal, she would be the woman who showed him life was worth living via activities like watching old Italian films on a laptop, eating fresh berries and running along the beach, laughing, while cutting their bare feet on seashells. She wouldn't mind turning herself into a cliché for love.

She left one of the female volunteers in charge, saying she was going on her lunch, though she had been already – it was near closing time for the museum. She followed him as he took off his gloves. A few blocks from the museum, he embraced a beautiful woman in a white cashmere coat and followed her into a pub. The woman was carrying a bouquet of yellow flowers.

They both had gin and tonics. Lil ordered a pint of dark beer after following them in.

He was not planning to kill her, or planning to kill himself because he hated her but couldn't leave her for some reason. Perhaps they had run away from some horrible situation, it was impossible for them to be together and so they would end their lives in Margate in a tragic embrace. She had no interest in saving or helping them as a unit. But their talk wasn't desperate. He said something in a transatlantic accent about trying out a vegan recipe he had seen online, and that he needed to pick up some leeks.

They left before Lil finished her beer. It was a whole meal in a glass, so she wouldn't waste it.

Lil carefully inspected the plants in her garden, the torn stems, the missing petals and berries. He wasn't some soulful intellectual murderer or would-be suicide case, but a shallow man, trying to prevent his beautiful wife or girlfriend's body being ruined by childbirth, by sneaking juniper berries and rue into ghastly, healthy recipes. Or maybe she *wanted* the abortions – was one of those women into holistic medicine and clean eating, sceptical of vaccinations – it was an agreement between them!

While Esme cut the flowers and put the leeks in the fridge, Tom said, 'My anxiety,' and locked himself in the bathroom. He had absentmindedly put one of his hands in his pockets, and it was itchy and red and he had to hide it. He used Esme's liquid foundation, smearing it on with his other hand. He blew on it, thinking it would dry instantly. The pain was agonising and his hand looked artificial.

The next time Tom went to the garden, Lil was waiting for him. She held him hostage in a quickly constructed cage of words outside the museum. 'You're not trying to give her miscarriages, you're trying to make her miscarry her own existence, to kill her, do her in. Walk to the sea with me.'

He walked slightly ahead of her, not listening.

'I have absurd dreams about a gigantic fountain being put on the sea here, to control it, to make it do more than just move back and forth,' she said, hoping to impress him, but he didn't even take in what she said, and she knew, deep down, that trying to inspire someone else, especially a man, was the laziest, most futile form of creativity. She also knew that while a man could seduce a woman with his art, a woman could never seduce a man with hers. The only way to make a man like that listen to her was to insult or offend him, the same way it took acid or vinegar to cut through a clogged drain.

'Your girlfriend looks like a jar of mayonnaise!' she yelled. 'If you take any more plants from my garden I'll have you arrested.'

He was amazed at what washed up on the shore in Margate. He saw a carrot once, and a round piece of gristle that could've been a previously hidden, obscure human body part. All the tiny shells, each one evidence of a death or abandonment.

In the poison garden, Lil picked everything, until she was holding armfuls. No one would use it again.

'This is my garden,' she said. 'Juniperus, atropa belladonna, aconitum, conium maculatum . . .'

The Surrogates

My boyfriend Taras and I were both aspiring writers desperate for money.

Our dream was to be able to switch working – that Taras could do it for a year while I wrote, and I would do it for a year as he wrote, and so on forever until we finished a stack of books each, but Taras's job was steady, and I had trouble holding on to one. Besides, we couldn't survive on one income – when I was without work it was difficult, and we could barely afford to eat and pay our rent.

Taras worked at a grocer's called the European Deli, at the meat, cheese and pickle counter. It was a very large shop on the other side of the city – Taras had to make an hour-long tram journey to get there and back. I was terrified he would slice his fingers on the meat slicer by accident, and wouldn't be able to write anymore, only dictate to me, pushing our dream even farther away as I would have to write out both of our books. Taras kept a notebook hidden under a hunk of roast beef, in which he wrote observations about customers to use in his 'novel in verse'.

Taras procured a sort of religious look of all black, often wearing long coats, with a golden cross on a chain, except at the European Deli where he had to wear a red shirt and an apron. He had a silver septum piercing and looked like a raging bull behind the counter, about to be slaughtered.

Taras sang in a men's Ukrainian choir which performed old Christian and folk songs – his main passion after writing his 'novel in verse'.

I liked the way Taras dressed so much that I imitated it. I bought a black hat, and trousers and combat boots and a black leather trench coat secondhand. I even got a silver holy cross earring, just as he wore in one ear. He kept his head shaved. I did it for him with a razor, carefully, as his skull was covered in moles, like some sort of rare speckled egg. My dark hair was streaked with white already.

For a while I worked in the kitchen of a restaurant as a dish washer, but the owner complained there were always specks of dried food left on the crockery I washed, which I just hadn't seen. I knew I needed glasses but I couldn't afford them.

I found a magnifying glass in a box of Taras's childhood things and brought it with me to work, inspecting the dishes for more dirt as I washed them, but I was fired for 'fooling around' and 'having my own possessions out at the workplace'. Taras had had the same glasses since he was a child, they barely fitted his face anymore, so he held them up like a pince-nez when reading. I once tried them on and got so dizzy I threw up.

I worked at a cinema for one day. I went into a screening to do an inspection and just sat down and watched the movie and forgot I was working. They sent me home after making me pay for a ticket. 'If it was a Krzysztof Kieślowski film, I would understand, but not a children's movie about a lost dog,' Taras said to me, which made me cry as my great-uncle had been in a Kieślowski film once long ago, then died at a young age from drinking too much.

Taras and I lived in a basement apartment that was all tiled. There were drain holes on the floors; the landlord said water sometimes came up. I think our apartment was just a giant bathtub. Perhaps it had once been a sauna, or a slaughterhouse. We weren't sure. I wasn't on the lease as the landlord told Taras he wouldn't rent to women, that a woman shouldn't live in such a place, but it was all we could afford.

On our bedroom wall we had a postcard of a young Mayakovsky, who Taras loved more than his namesake, Taras Shevchenko, whom he found too sentimental though he was embarrassed to love a Russian poet over a Ukrainian one. Taras's ancestors were Ukrainian farmers who'd moved to the prairies of Canada in the nineteenth century.

My parents were Polish. Beside Taras's Mayakovsky postcard, I had a picture of the poet Zbigniew Herbert and a glittery illustration of Saint Francis with a baby deer at his feet and birds on his shoulders. Taras said I was a hypocrite because I loved to eat ham and tripe and Saint Francis was the patron saint of animals. The pictures were all crumpled as they often fell off the wall due to the damp, and we slept on them by accident.

Taras brought me large Polish hams, dappled like walnuts, cherry-flavoured chocolate bars, cheesecake and my favourite brand of juice which had a cartoon bear on the package, as he got a discount at the European Deli.

Taras built a bed for us on stilts, and we placed chairs and stools all around the apartment so we could jump around without getting our feet wet when the water rose, pungent, dark and strangely foamy. We left the bottom two shelves of each bookcase empty after losing some of our favourite novels.

I decided to become a surrogate so we could buy new copies.

We knew I was fertile enough to be a surrogate because a few months before, I'd had an abortion. The hospital just gave us a kit to do it, but didn't tell us how to dispose of the zygote. Taras said that if we buried it then the logic was that we believed it was actually a child, so we just threw it in the compost bins of a community allotment garden nearby, which we didn't have plots at because the waiting list was too long. We tried to grow potatoes in pots around our apartment, but it was too dark, even for potatoes.

The couple we were matched with through a surrogate ad were called the Reids. They smelled like boiled peas to me, and both had reddish yellow hair, as if they had dipped blond hair in blood. They did not want to use my eggs and would pay a large sum for us to carry their fertilised egg, which was inserted into me in a hospital. Taras came with me. One of the nurses at the hospital thought he was a monk praying for me because of his cross necklace, and he was so flattered that his whole head turned pink. I lived in fear Taras would abandon me for a monastery in Greece where women were not allowed to roam.

When they inserted the egg, I closed my eyes and imagined the nurse sticking a big chicken's egg on a silver spoon into my body.

The Reids found us a small house between a garage and an abandoned clothing factory. It had an upstairs and a downstairs, and a cellar Taras discovered through a linoleum-covered hatch in the kitchen, which was a different pattern of linoleum from the rest of the floor. We put all of our new books on the second floor, just in case – we were too used to the floods. The Reids told us they were renting it solely for the duration of the pregnancy, to protect the fetus from damp vapours, and we had to be out in nine months.

The floorboards of the house were rough, and I got a gigantic splinter in my foot which bled a lot when Taras took it out. I wore several pairs of socks when the Reids visited so they wouldn't notice the wound. Otherwise, we both agreed the house was swell.

Each week we had a grocery box delivered from the Reids, which always contained the same things: a large bottle of milk, turnips and carrots, veal, white fish, a can of sweetcorn, plain yogurt, Edam cheese, gravy powder, a bag of mealy green apples.

'That is not what a pregnant woman should eat,' said Taras. 'She should eat borscht, black tea and liver.'

We used what we could of the food they gave us and threw out the rest, eating as regular. We didn't think the Reids would find out, but they did after I had to give a urine sample to the doctor at a pregnancy checkup. My urine was red from eating beets.

After that, the Reids came over every night for dinner and cooked for us. They would not allow me sugar, alcohol, fermented things, caffeine or anything that was carcinogenic, which they said included ham, smoked fish and hot dogs.

I dreamed they boiled me this strange white turtle, with no head and dozens of legs, to eat, but when I poked it with my fork it got up off my plate and scuttled away, out of the dining room and into the hall, steam still rising from its back.

The Reids brought their boiled pea smell with them, and neither Taras nor I could smoke in the house with them around or speak in our own invented language, a mixture of Ukrainian, Polish and English.

In the evenings, after Taras got home from work, we liked to listen to Mussorgsky while smoking cigarettes, eat dumplings or go for long walks, which we could no longer do with the Reids around all the time.

The Reids removed Taras's David Bowie and Duran Duran records – they thought the song 'A View to a Kill' rather wicked, and said, 'It's just temporary, for our fetus,' telling us that if they couldn't make minor adjustments to our lifestyle they would have to take us to live in their house, which we dreaded as we imagined it to have wall-to-wall yellow carpets, microwaves and a television on all the time. The next time the Reids came over, Taras hid all of our books.

Mr Reid liked to sing British sailor songs we didn't know to the fetus, moving his knee up and down as he did so and making his voice extra loud to penetrate the layers of skin, muscle and fat of my stomach. Mrs Reid brought along knitting – little white jumpers. They both had weak chins, so it was like having two sock puppets chat to me. I imagined them taking off my trousers and trying to stick their small weak heads up my vagina to check on their child.

On the nights Taras had Ukrainian choir, I was left alone with the Reids, who prodded my stomach and watched me eat boiled chicken and sweetcorn.

I imagined a small child belonging to Taras and me growing around their big, pink, leech-like baby, thin and wrinkled and with no access to food. I felt more and more like I was connected to the Reids in a gross sexual way too, especially after they had made polite insinuations that Taras and I shouldn't sleep together lest it hurt or disturb the fetus. The insinuations were enough to put me off sex.

Taras borrowed a giant, blood-spattered calculator from the deli counter and calculated the amount we were being paid vs the amount of time we were having to spend with the Reids, and it didn't seem like enough anymore. 'We could have perhaps finished our novels and sold them, even – it's not out of the question,' he said, which made us both feel gloomy.

I had not got much writing done on my experimental novel *Hunky Dory Eugene* because I felt sick, tired and bloated, and also guilty that mine wasn't a real job in the way that Taras's was, especially because the Reids hadn't given us any money yet.

I imagined my stomach solid and pink all the way through like a big round ham, and that the Reids would one day come and slice it off and carry it away. I wanted them to do it soon, but we had three more months to go.

'I have an idea,' said Taras. 'We'll disappear, and send them a ransom letter: triple the price and they can have the baby.'

We left very early one morning, knapsacks filled with our books and snacks, to take the bus to Winnipeg, where Taras's brother lived. His parents lived there too, but we didn't want them to see that I was pregnant. Taras had told the European Deli he had to go see his uncle, who'd been in a farming accident.

It was a thirty-hour bus ride – we couldn't afford an airplane or train. The seats of the bus were dirty and grey like mice, and the toilet at the back of the bus smelled like very old urine.

Taras sat with his big arms around me. We had read on the news that on the same bus journey, a man had once eaten the head of the person sitting beside him, so we made sure to sit with two or three seats between us and the other passengers. Taras had stolen a knife from the European Deli and hid it in his trousers. I kept accidentally stroking it.

We munched on ham and toffees, and Taras told me his brother worked at a popcorn factory which only made pink popcorn – the mascot was a sad clown with a rectangular body and candy cane arms. Perhaps, he said, we could both get jobs there, though the pay was low

('My brother survives on popcorn from the factory floor and cheese dumplings') and Winnipeg was so windy we would both have to get fur coats.

As we came into Winnipeg, a woman in her snowy yard opened her big winter coat and flashed us as we drove past – she was naked underneath and her breasts were blue. She cackled, though we couldn't hear it through the bus window, only see it.

We wrote to the Reids once we got off the bus.

We slept on Taras's brother's couch, in his small bungalow, the wind howling outside. There was a large Ukrainian flag on the wall of the living room, blindingly yellow and blue, and bits of pink popcorn, like torn pieces of flesh, here and there on the floor.

A few days after we arrived, we received a letter back from the Reids in response to our ransom. Taras read it out loud to me.

'They say they are relieved we took off, because the latest hospital tests revealed the fetus to be "retarded".' He paused.

'They say that they also implanted a fertilised egg in a woman in a hospital in Uganda, where they chain the surrogates to the beds, keep the doors locked and feed them according to the parents' wishes, and that fetus is in much better condition.'

Madame Flora's

Victoria's menses stopped. Her nanny looked through her old nappy bustles, the ones that hadn't been thrown away yet, and it had not arrived when it was supposed to. Her nanny checked the diary she kept of Victoria's menses ('Light', 'Regular', 'Thick', 'An Odd Smell'). Each sentence was accompanied by a fingerprint of blood, from the moment little Victoria, aged thirteen, held up a bloody hand saying, 'Nanny, I'm dying,' to which Nanny replied that the nappy bustle Victoria had always worn was in preparation for such bleeding and that the bleeding was best called *blooming* and the blood best called *flowers* by a young lady.

Ladies wore nappy bustles all the time so men wouldn't know exactly when they were menstruating. It was less obscene that way, the constant taffeta swish-swish of the nappies that accompanied women's movements giving no indication of their cycle. They were large and scented, made out of cotton and plastic. Women past the age of menstruating still wore them, as did little girls, so there was no sense of end or beginning. The bustles were reassuring: women would never leak. Women were like eggs made out of marble, not creatures made of meat.

Nanny told Victoria's mother, who told Victoria's father that Victoria was dreadfully weakened. Victoria's father called the family doctor, who, upon hearing that Victoria's periods had stopped, hurried over with a bottle of Madame Flora's, which he handed to Victoria's father, saying that he saw this affliction all the time in young ladies and it was nothing to worry about.

'It's such a horror, the idea of flowers from a woman's body. It seems a shame to bring it back when it has disappeared,' Victoria's father said, with the abstract disgust of a man who had never seen it before.

The doctor laughed. 'It is indeed, but it is a necessity of life.'

The bottle was made of milky green glass: opaque, so the liquid inside wasn't visible.

They all knew of Madame Flora's. Madame Flora's was 'The Number One Cure for Weakness, Nervous Complaints, Fainting and Dizziness'. Her advertisements were everywhere, on billboards and magazines, illustrations of fainted ladies contrasted with ones of ladies dancing and carrying children. Ladies sitting on half-moons, laughing, bouquets of blossoming flowers. In many shopping arcades there was a mechanical wax girl in a glass box, eternally consuming Madame Flora's. When the bottle reached her mouth, a blush spread through her wax cheeks.

Victoria's father opened the bottle and took a strong sniff, then another. He stuck his finger in and when he pulled it out, it was coated with a dense, dark brown syrup. The bottle label suggested mixing it with tonic water, or putting it in puddings or spreading it on toast with butter.

Nanny tried a spoonful herself. The doctor and Victoria's father looked away with slight revulsion.

She spat it into her hand then wiped her hand on her apron.

'Sir, it tastes of . . . bloo—'

'Nonsense. It's a one hundred per cent herbal mixture, I have read the label and prescribed it to many patients. I would not expect you to know what blood tastes like,' said the doctor.

'I only know, sir, from the smell of it.'

Victoria's father grabbed the bottle and looked for the ingredients, but they weren't listed.

In small letters at the bottom of the label it said, *For Extreme Cases, Please Consider a Holiday at Madame Flora's Hotel.*

The doctor, Victoria's father and Nanny went up to Victoria's bedroom.

The canopy curtains of Victoria's bed were closed. Nanny opened them. Victoria lay in bed, reading a book of nursery rhymes and smoking. Her long red hair was greasy-looking. Nanny grabbed her cigarette and put it out under her boot.

'Nanny!' Victoria cried.

The doctor and Victoria's father chuckled.

Nanny prepared a glass of Madame Flora's in the bedroom kitchenette. Women weren't allowed in the main kitchens of houses, but the kitchenette was a place where they could prepare light meals – there was an electric tea kettle, and a tiny plastic oven, which used a light bulb and was decorated with flowers, that could warm toast and make little cakes but never burn anything. There were boxes of powders that could be turned into various porridges, tea, malt powder and seaweed jelly powder and always a fresh bottle of milk.

Victoria tried to spit out the Madame Flora's but Nanny stopped her. She swallowed with a grimace. 'Bring me a crumpet, Nanny, and some milk to chase it down, please, Nanny.'

'Be quiet, Victoria,' said her father.

'Bring the child some milk,' said the doctor. 'The taste of Madame Flora's is not delicate.'

Victoria was to be given Madame Flora's in the morning, at lunchtime and before bed. She complained that Madame Flora's gave her fevers and constipation. She rinsed her mouth out after taking it, and often went to the bathroom, sticking two of her fingers down her throat until she vomited it up. She did everything she could to get Madame Flora's out of her body. She didn't miss her menses, the gelatinous clots that reminded her of leeches, the fear of leaks even when she wore chafing rubber underwear under her bustle.

They tried the whole range of Madame Flora's products. In addition to the tonic, they sold pastilles, pills, powders, bouillon squares for soup and a line of chocolate-covered Madame Flora's jelly that looked like Turkish delight but tasted like rust, sulphur and browned flowers.

Victoria poured Madame Flora's on the crotch of her nappy bustle hoping it would pass, but Nanny knew.

Victoria's father said he would send her to Madame Flora's Hotel.

'Can't Nanny come with me to Madame Flora's?' Victoria asked.

'No, she must look after your mother,' her father said, and Victoria was secretly pleased, for she wanted to be away from Nanny.

They took the carriage. Victoria wore a green taffeta dress. Besides her trunk, she had a small black velvet purse, inside which were love letters from her father's butler and one of her father's friends. One contained a dried daisy, stuck to the page with horse glue.

Victoria's mother brought a large tin of wine gums along for the ride, keeping it on her lap. They were all she would eat, the blackcurrant-flavoured ones in particular.

Her father brought cold roast beef, a spiral sausage that resembled a round rag rug, and pâté along for himself. He didn't stop to eat it but let the smell fill up the whole carriage. 'I feel so ill I want to die,' Victoria said to herself. Women weren't allowed to eat meat. The smell of it was intolerably strong.

They had to stop twice, for forty minutes each time, so her father could go to the lavatory. There were men smoking and loitering outside the men's WCs. On a bench by the bathroom door, there was a man with swollen-looking red legs, his trousers rolled up to reveal them. He was eating potted meat with his fingers and grinning. There was a smell around the place, like burnt mutton, and her mother held a handkerchief to her face as they waited. 'Why do men take ever so long to toilet?' asked Victoria, and her mother told her not to be vulgar, drooling as she spoke because of the wine gums.

Victoria knew the right amount she could piss in her bustle without it leaking or smelling. She did so. There weren't many public bathrooms for women.

Madame Flora's Hotel overlooked the sea. It was a white building, like most in the town, which was a popular seaside resort. The words 'Madame Flora's' were written in large gold letters and there was a billboard on the roof of the hotel with an image of Madame Flora's tonic, surrounded by roses. The main doors were glass with golden bars. The veranda had no chairs, only large potted ferns.

The hotel foyer smelled of the bouquets of flowers placed on countertops and desks, but the floor was overrun with suitcases, tennis rackets and other sports equipment. In the centre of the foyer was an enormous, strong-looking young woman wearing a fur coat, her dark hair in braided loops pinned to her head. In one hand she held a lacrosse stick. There was a vase knocked over in front of her, the water turning the red carpet a darker shade.

'I want my own room,' the girl said loudly.

'If ladies are in a room together, their flowers will blossom together,' said a woman in a purple dress with red frills and a matching hat.

'I don't understand what you're saying,' replied the girl. 'Where am I to put all my things?'

'It is beneficial to becoming well again. It is our policy,' the woman said and turned to Victoria and her family.

'A moment alone with the young lady, please,' she said, curtsying to the parents and taking Victoria's arm and bringing her behind the hotel counter into a small room.

The woman had a fob watch hanging down her skirt: this was Madame Flora. Her bustle was huge. She looked like a dining-room chair from the side. She wore a small glass vial on a necklace which she said was full of Madame Flora's, from one of the first bottles she had made. The liquid looked dried, dark and old.

There wasn't a desk in the room, only a matching set of patterned couches, a drink service on wheels with crystal glasses and tonic, and a few little side tables with more flowers on them, along with some porcelain figurines and plaster fruit. Madame Flora shut the door and told Victoria to sit down. The walls were covered in photographs and drawings of babies. 'From former guests at Madame Flora's, once their flowers returned,' she said. 'Madame Flora's is available for anyone to purchase, but our hotel is reserved for the most exclusive of clientele. I take a personal interest in all the guests here. Madame Flora's is made in a factory in the north where the water is strong, but I prefer to be here, with the girls who need my help most.'

She paused to smile at Victoria, revealing rust-stained teeth.

'And do you like taking your Madame Flora's?'

Victoria would've blushed, if she'd had the energy, but she knew her cheeks remained pale and slightly green.

'I don't like it. It feels like a poison, I don't like it going into my body,' said Victoria.

'Well, medicine isn't supposed to be tasty, now, is it?' Madame Flora said.

She poured a glass of her tonic and handed it to Victoria. Under her gaze, Victoria drank it.

'It is a policy here that girls share rooms, as you may have heard.'

Victoria's mother handed her a wine gum wrapped in a tissue as they said goodbye.

The girl from the foyer was named Louise and she was the daughter of a baron. She was assigned the same room as Victoria. They weren't allowed to take the stairs, only the lift. The stairs were gated off, and through the bars Victoria could see the layer of dust that covered the red carpet staircase. Victoria was afraid Louise would make the lift break with all her things. There were only three floors, and the halls had dim lights and were stuffy.

Their room was on the top floor, filled with small but pretty beds with rose-patterned bed sheets. There were lots of small mirrors, and bedside tables with powders and Madame Flora's on them. There was a marble fireplace, lit, with a decorative brass fireguard in front of it, and potpourri in little china dishes. There was a small window looking out onto the sea, and a skylight. One wall had a mural of Mother Goose on it. A small pink door led to a bathroom. There was an indent on the far side of the room with a curtain across it, which Louise pulled back, revealing another bed. In it lay a thin girl with pale blonde hair and a red scalp, holding a paper box to her chest. She wore a wrinkled, cream-coloured nightgown.

'I was here first,' the girl said quietly, not looking at her intruder.

Louise pushed one of the beds under the skylight and, standing on it, tapped it with her lacrosse stick.

A few more girls came into the room through the door, carrying carpet bags, hats and other belongings. One with black hair who took the bed beside Victoria was named Eliza, and a girl with curls was named Matilda. None of them had shared a room with so many girls before.

They wandered around their small room, touching things. In the fireplace there was a bit of a stocking and a burnt crumpet. On the wall, behind Victoria's metal bed frame, someone had scrawled 'Mutton'. There was a collage on the wall, of horses and dogs, badly cut out of newspapers. In the bathroom was a framed picture of a lady riding a rabbit.

Without looking at any of the girls in particular, Louise talked, taking off her coat. Her dress had a sailor's bib and a strange cut, with low hips, which wasn't suited to her bustle. The sleeves were short. On one arm she had a Union Jack tattoo, which the other girls thought shocking until Louise said her father had it done to her when she was eight, which meant her father loved her very much.

'After this I'm going to Fairy Palace, in Wales, to fix my teeth. My Hugh had his teeth fixed there. Then we are getting married.'

She suddenly looked at Victoria.

'Are they going to send you somewhere to fix your nose next?'

Victoria covered her nose with one of her hands.

Louise continued talking. 'They've fixed my hymen twice now – both times it broke from riding horses. It has to be intact just before you're married so that a nurse hired by your fiancé can break it with a metal instrument. It's so he won't be put off by the sight of blood after the wedding. Your fiancé gets a certificate from the nurse saying it was done.' Victoria didn't understand what a hymen was – perhaps a little male China doll? Victoria's dolls had never bled, though she often checked and made them nappies out of tissue.

Louise pointed to the collage of dogs and horses. 'It's shaped like the Kingdom of Wales.'

'No it isn't – I'm from Wales,' said Eliza. Louise slapped her.

There was a nappy bustle dispensary: a tin box hung on the wall. Louise pulled out nappy bustles, throwing them into the room until they were called for dinner. The dining room was full of small round tables, and only two or three girls could fit at each. There were many older women there, who were married, and they were in separate, individual rooms. It made Louise angry. 'Bitches,' she said. They spent most of their time playing cards in the parlour or writing long letters to their husbands and children.

There were large bottles of Madame Flora's, surrounded by tiny bottles and oranges as table centrepieces. Oranges were said to help with the constipation that too much Madame Flora's could cause. They were served bowls of mashed potatoes with sugar and milk, or bowls of white bread with sugar and milk, cups of tea with sugar and cream, and more oranges; there were bowls of peeled oranges and orange jelly, crumpets, tiny pots of jam, cabbage and boiled carrots, rice pudding. Victoria sat with a pudgy girl with dark circles under her eyes who said, quietly, 'I've not stopped my flowers for the same reason as everyone else. Have you ever been in love?'

Victoria thought of her father, her father's butler, and her father's friends, and said, 'No.' The girl ate too much cabbage and rice pudding and had wind. She told Victoria that she knew a girl whose flowers stopped after she saw a dead man in a ditch, but she was cured at Madame Flora's, and that she herself would never be cured, which she said with a little giggle Victoria didn't like.

After dinner, the girls were told to go to bed. Rest was the most important thing. Louise stuck a photo of Hugh, a real lock of his blond hair glued to it like a toupee, in the middle of the dog and horse collage. 'He has more dogs and horses than all that,' she said.

Louise's hands were surprisingly dainty and pudgy, with expensive feminine rings, including her engagement ring from Hugh Orville. Her nails were polished, red and sharp like vole's teeth.

Hugh Orville turned up the next day. Madame Flora wouldn't let him visit, but he left gifts for Louise – a stuffed toy swan, a box of chocolates. He drove around the hotel grounds in his motor car playing a popular song Louise loved called 'Tinky Tinky Too Too', a duet between a trumpet and a theremin. Louise moved from window to window, waving and dancing. Hugh was stunningly handsome. He wore a blue kerchief and a fur coat like Louise's, flashing his new teeth from Fairy Palace. Louise told everyone he was a duke.

Eliza had several black dresses, all velvet or silk. They all looked similar but she wore the same one every day and every night until it smelled, merely changing her stockings and bustle discreetly in the morning.

Matilda's dresses were exceptionally ugly, Louise told Victoria. They were of calico, brown, mustard yellow, pink.

Each girl had her own way of taking Madame Flora's, of standing the nasty taste. Eliza liked to mix Madame Flora's with black tea, Matilda with tonic water, so it was weakened. She would only put a drop or two in. Victoria copied her. The girl who slept behind the curtain and wouldn't say her name put it in milk, so that it was a pink colour. Many in the dining room put it in their porridge.

Louise took a straight teaspoon in the morning, with lunch and before bed, without complaining or grimacing.

She had an iron ball which she licked and threatened to throw at the other girls. Her nanny at home had given her the ball as an anaemia cure, and she was addicted to it, but Madame Flora took it away saying it was bad for her, as were greens. 'Spinach is poisonous. My tonic is the only safe source of iron for women.'

Each evening, a maid came and took away their nappy bustles and dirty laundry in a cart, and examined the bed sheets and blankets for stains. It didn't feel as cruel as when Nanny did it, tutting and sighing. There were simply so many girls at Madame Flora's. It wasn't personal.

Louise, who wore pyjamas instead of a nightie to bed, talked into the night. There was nothing else to do, besides reading magazines.

'I saw a man eating a boiled egg, he grinned at me as he done so.'

'I sniffed a rasher of bacon, once, in the kitchen at home.'

'Hugh killed eight pheasants and a fox last spring.'

There was a middle-aged woman who sat herself in the lift and wouldn't come out. Others squished buns through the brass grating to make her eat but she wouldn't let anyone pour any Madame Flora's in; she called it devil's juice. She wasn't married. Madame Flora put some of her concoction in a spray bottle and sprayed the woman with it but she turned around and crouched in a far corner of the lift. Madame told them to ignore her and look away when they passed. There were queues for the one remaining lift. The woman screamed and shook the lift during the night and silently paced during the day. Louise spat orange pips at her whenever she passed by the lift.

One morning they came down and the lift was empty and clean again.

On his second visit, Hugh brought Louise a miniature golf set which she set up in the parlour.

'Exercise is the enemy of your flowers, Louise,' Madame Flora said, taking Louise's golf club as she took a swing. This made Louise so despondent that Madame Flora made an effort to provide entertainment. Victoria couldn't see how Louise could be bored. There were so many ladies' magazines to read at Madame Flora's – *The Modern Priscilla*, *Dainty Day*, *News for Ladies* – in big stacks everywhere. Victoria's nanny had sent her some popular poems on card paper that she had written out herself in brown ink. Victoria ripped them up. She was scared of Nanny visiting Madame Flora's like Hugh did, of Nanny circling the hotel crying, 'Victoria, Victoria!'

Madame Flora took the girls about town.

The town was full of hotels, shopping arcades, stalls selling postcards, seashell art ('Don't touch the seashells, girls!' said Madame Flora) and novelty tea sets with the Royal Family on them. There were rides and other amusements. Madame Flora hired a long, covered rickshaw pulled by two cyclists to take the girls around. The seats were very small, and made of metal. Louise struggled to fit in one, so she balanced herself on the back of the seat, her legs hanging down the arms. She harassed the cyclists, telling them to go faster, or slow down when she saw something that looked amusing, especially the butcher shops which had striped curtains covering the windows and signs that said 'Gentlemen Only'. 'What do they sell, eh?' she muttered. 'Sausage. Eggs. Snouts.'

Victoria half covered her ears to make herself look good in front of Madame Flora, but was intrigued by what Louise was saying. Louise could only be distracted from the butcher shops by a carousel on one of the piers.

Madame Flora said yes to a ride, and made one of the maids run back to the hotel and get some soft padding to put on the fake animals before the girls sat on them. 'Sideways, girls, sideways, like you do properly on a horse.'

Once she'd checked all the girls were rightly seated, she nodded to the carousel owner, but after it had gone round a few times, Louise changed positions on her zebra, so both legs hung down different sides. She had taken her bustle off and sent it flying. It resembled a swan as it fell into the seawater. Madame Flora shouted for the carousel to stop. By the time it did, Louise had wrapped her legs around the pole of the zebra, laughing wildly.

Madame Flora didn't let them go out any more after that, saying it would use up the energy needed to restore their flowers. Someone came and gave a lecture on ferns, bringing samples in misty glass jars.

'I don't want my flowers again, ever, I just want to get out of here. I never want babies,' muttered Matilda, touching one of the glass jars.

Madame Flora could tell at a glance the difference between menstrual blood and blood from a wound.

When Matilda told the maids she had her flowers again, and held up her sheets, Madame Flora came in and pulled up Matilda's nightgown, exposing her nappy bustle. Her legs and stomach were covered in small cuts.

'How could you do this to yourself, sweetest of hearts? We just want to help you get better. Don't we treat you well?' asked Madame Flora. They examined her for cuts each week. They put bandages over the ones she had and checked to make sure she didn't rip them off and reopen the wounds.

As Louise continued to be restless, Madame Flora hired two performers: a couple with their small dog, who wore fancy hats and sang and danced and were popular in all the seaside towns. Madame Flora placed a velvet railing to separate the girls from the couple, and Louise made them sing 'Tinky Tinky Too Too' twice, stomping her foot along so loudly the floor shook. Everyone was relieved to see Louise entertained, but the couple's dog had gone missing by the end of the show and they caused a fuss Madame Flora thought to be upsetting to her clients.

'Doggy, doggy!' they cried. 'Where is our doggy?' The man begged Madame Flora to let him carry around a piece of cheese to lure it out from wherever it was hiding. Madame Flora told them they were disgusting and made them leave without payment.

'Must have got out,' said Louise. 'Must have drowned in the sea.'

Victoria thought once they were in their bedroom Louise would pull the dog out from under her dress, but she didn't. 'I'm not interested in mutts,' she said. Hugh had basset hounds, corgis and Dutch partridge dogs that he imported from the Netherlands despite the heavy taxation. They could hear the couple shouting outside the hotel: 'Where is our doggy? Bitch, bitch!'

A few days later the dog was found dead in one of the halls. Madame Flora was livid at the thought that there was now 'meat' in her establishment, the hall was cordoned off, and the girls heard she burnt the dog in the kitchen oven. Victoria wondered if she was afraid to put it in the rubbish. The smell of burnt fur and flesh wafted up through all the rooms, and Madame Flora filled her establishment with electric fans and more bowls of potpourri.

None of the girls told Madame Flora about the time, in the chaos of getting up and getting dressed, a sausage had rolled out onto the floor of their bedroom. At first they'd thought it was a dried turd.

Louise picked it up and ate it before Madame Flora and one of the maids entered the room, having heard their screams.

No one knew who'd left the sausage, except it couldn't have been Louise because she would have eaten it beforehand. She ate things as soon as she received them because she knew she would always get more.

There was no change in Louise's pallor after eating the sausage, nor was she sick. All the girls that had been in the room watched her closely.

'What about girls who have too much?' Victoria asked in the dark, in bed one night.

'Too much what?'

'You know, too many flowers.'

No one replied, except for Louise, who said, 'You need a licence stating you are male to buy meat, but I once heard about a woman who dressed up as a man and bought a rack of lamb and was arrested. Maybe the girls who had too many flowers were arrested too.' Louise chuckled loudly, and the sound filled the room like a horrid fart.

'Or died because they didn't have anything left in their bodies,' said Matilda. 'Maybe their hearts came out with their flowers.'

After some silence, Eliza whispered, 'There was a boy, Thomas, he loved me. He cut himself, on his arm, and let me drink the blood; he did it a number of times, on his legs and his arms, he said it didn't count as meat and I started to get better, but he died of infection from one of the cuts.'

A week later, Louise was standing on a chair below the skylight, shouting, 'In here!' It was one of the rickshaw cyclists. Louise had sent him a message through one of the maids, perhaps. 'Open the latch,' she growled.

He had put on cologne and it filled the room. He had sweat stains under the armpits of his beige suit, a fresh and red young face and a little moustache that had been waxed and curled with care.

He took off his trousers and underpants but left on his jacket, shirt, bow tie, shoes and socks. He lay on his side on Eliza's bed, looking at them all and making kissing sounds. Eliza got up and sat beside Victoria, clutching her arm. 'I want her to do it,' he said, pointing to Eliza.

'Sit up,' she said to him, and he did, spreading his legs wide. She went in-between.

He winced, but they couldn't see what was going on – her head was in the way. The man moaned.

'His thingy's in her ear,' whispered Louise. Eliza turned around, blood on her lips. The man's thing was all sweaty and there was blood all over his thigh, where she had bitten. Louise went over but he said, 'I'll come back tomorrow night,' and zipped up his trousers, seeming not to think of the blood, as if he didn't know he had been bitten.

There was a bandage over the bite when he returned.

'The other thigh,' he said.

Louise didn't bite, but tried to use her nail scissors. The man screamed and said, 'No, use your lips and teeth.' She did, but made a show of cleaning her face off with a hanky and perfume afterwards, and all the other girls knew it was because he was working class.

The girl from behind the curtain came out and drank some too. Matilda and Victoria didn't.

'Bring a friend tomorrow then,' Louise said to the man as he left.

The young man didn't come back the next night, but another came and knew what would happen, taking off his trousers too. After Eliza and Louise drank, Matilda took off her bustle, climbed up on the man, sitting on him, and moved around in an odd manner that made the man giggle and whelp.

'What are you doing?' said Louise.

'I don't want any blood,' said Matilda in a breathy voice. 'I just want to keep doing what I'm doing.'

Louise scowled and, grabbing one of the man's arms, made a cut in it and started drinking. He barely noticed. His other arm reached up and grabbed Matilda's breast, squeezing. It looked like it must have hurt to Victoria.

The next night, a different man came, and the same thing happened. Matilda sat on him while the other girls cut him and drank from him like a fountain in a garden. 'But I don't want my flowers,' said Victoria to herself, watching. The girl from behind the curtain copied Matilda and sat on the man too. Matilda said if you didn't have your flowers, you could do it all you want and you wouldn't have any children. All the other girls laughed, confused, except for Louise who said, 'Hugh wants twenty children,' in a serious voice. Later in the night, Victoria woke to the sound of Louise trying to do with a pillow what Matilda did with the men.

They accumulated left-behind socks, bow ties, shirts, jackets, trousers, shoes, suspenders. One man left his underpants, which Louise used as a nightcap. The girls tried them all on, taking turns, their bustles lying around the room like gigantic broken eggshells. How easy it was to become men.

'I could walk into a butcher shop and buy myself a piece of ham,' said Eliza.

One young man fainted after they drank his blood. Louise slapped him, and they poured Madame Flora's down his throat. He sputtered, and sat up, then vomited up the Madame Flora's all down the front of his suit.

'I'm bleeding again,' the girl from behind her curtain said weakly one morning.

'Wonderful, delightful,' said Madame Flora when she entered, looking at the bleeding girl. On closer inspection, however, her smile disappeared. She called for one of the maids. Together, they carried the girl out of the room, blood dripping from her nightgown.

Hugh stopped by the hotel again to drop off a gigantic basket of fruit, including a pineapple and three bananas. Louise ate too much and got diarrhoea. She drank Madame Flora's straight from the bottle to stop it.

'I'll just have a small taste,' said Victoria, next time a man came. Eliza was on one arm, Louise on the other, and Matilda was sitting on him. Victoria made a cut on his foot. Blood tasted like a fresh version of Madame Flora's, she thought.

At the end, they couldn't wake the man up from his faint. They poured Madame Flora's on his face but he didn't respond.

'He can sleep behind the curtain till he's better,' said Victoria.

'He's dead,' responded Louise. 'He's meat now.'

They put him in Louise's trunk.

All the blood from the man must have gone into Louise because her flowers started soon after. Wearing her stained pyjamas, she ran down into the foyer to use the telephone box. Everyone in the hotel could hear her shouting into it, 'FLOWERS, HUGH, FLOWERS!' A few hours later a carriage from her parents' house arrived, followed by Hugh Orville in a motor car.

Louise took the trunk with the man inside with her. 'I'll take care of it,' she said to the other girls.

Her wedding was in all the papers a few weeks later. She had new teeth too, which looked exactly the same as Hugh's. They both made sure to show the teeth off in the photos.

Eliza left soon after. She said she wished Thomas could see her flowers, which was a wicked thing to say even though he was dead. No one would ever now, she supposed, unless she had to come back to Madame Flora's. She didn't have a nanny at home.

'Give me a spot of yours,' Matilda begged Eliza. She didn't just spread it in her bustle, but inside herself and on her legs too. It even tricked Madame Flora.

Victoria was left alone, except for the picture of Hugh that Louise had left behind.

I'll be in and out of here for the rest of my life, Victoria thought, I'll be stopping and starting my flowers, I'll be spitting up Madame Flora's, I'll settle here forever with the parlour wives.

There were leftover Madame Flora bottles all over the room. She poured the contents of them into the toilet, without flushing, and giggled as she did so. Then she sat on one of the beds and opened a magazine. On the cover was a woman using a telephone, her spare hand sitting atop a bouquet of roses.

The Coiled Serpent

Three young men lived in a very long top-floor apartment together. It stretched across three or four buildings. There were a few holes in the ceiling, it was draughty, the kitchen and bathroom were mere skeletons of a kitchen and a bathroom, but they wanted to save money, though they all had positions at the Intl Computer Company.

They worked in the windowless basement of the company, as programmers. The computer system took up three rooms, large humming machines with different-sized monitors here and there, displaying bright green information.

They had one personal computer at home, not larger than a microwave, which one of them – Pax – built, and they all fiddled around on it when they had new ideas.

At an army surplus shop they had purchased three narrow camp beds to sleep on in different sections of the attic. They also got cheap forks, knives and bowls, striped Russian navy shirts which protected against the cold, water bottles and olive-coloured rucksacks for their hikes and adventures.

Pax and Angelo had also purchased Japanese screens with cranes on them from a specialist shop to give some degree of privacy, while Alexander, satisfied that the other two had them, decided he did not need one himself. Alexander's bed was surrounded by piles of books (*The Golden Bough, Computer Lib/Dream Machines, Gödel, Escher, Bach: An Eternal Golden Braid, The Letters of Pliny the Younger, The World as Will and Idea, Beyond Good and Evil,* a Bible, *The Odyssey, Moby-Dick, Crime and Punishment, A Hero of Our Time, Walden, Brave New World, Collected Works of John Keats et al*), a pair of iron dumbbells, a small Greek imitation vase which he used as an ashtray, and a cassette player. He had two tapes, Roxy Music's *Avalon* and the single 'City Lights' by William Pitt. These he listened to while he lifted his dumbbells, every morning and night, before and after work.

Every night for dinner, Alexander had a steak with a tinned pineapple ring on top, and for breakfast, a gallon of cow's milk, or occasionally goat's, though the goat's milk bottles smelled and Angelo complained. Alexander wanted to drink human breast milk as it was the healthiest, and took out ads in various newspapers asking to buy some, but no one replied to his adverts. He never ate lunch, just brought one of his bottles of milk to work with three peeled garlic cloves which he chewed slowly throughout the day.

In their fridge, along with all of Alexander's milk and steak, and various sauces belonging to Pax, there was a cloudy jar of brine which contained a single headless curl of fish.

'Are you going to eat that pickled herring, Angelo?' Pax said every now and then, rubbing his stomach. 'I have nothing to put on my sandwich but chutney and prawn crackers.'

'No – fuck off, Pax, will you.'

When no one else was home, Angelo took the jar into the bathroom, along with a small box of toothpicks. He took the herring piece out and stuck it together, in a loop, with one of the toothpicks to a perfect size for his penis and masturbated by moving it up and down the tip. After he came, he threw the toothpick out and put the herring back into the jar, back in the fridge.

On one of the ground floors below them was a Sichuan restaurant. Once a month they went there for dinner. Alexander always drank too much of the complimentary green tea and had to piss all night and Pax always ordered the spiciest thing.

Pax liked to buy bags of prawn crackers from them to take home, though Alexander told him they were all air and no protein. Angelo liked to melt chocolate bars, chilli sauce and slices of cheese together in a pot. Once it had hardened into a candle-like texture, he ate it in chunks and called it power food. He also had a vast collection of teas in tins, canisters and boxes, loose tea whose leaves stuck between his teeth when he drank it. There were teas to concentrate, to strengthen, to stay awake, to cure hangovers, to go to sleep. There were packages with geishas on them, others with mice wearing nightcaps and some with wise, old-looking men with tremendously long beards. The different teas tasted like aluminium, flowers, perfume, dog shit, beef.

Pax had a beard with a stripe of white in it which he dyed black but it was always blacker looking than the rest of his beard, which was really just dark brown.

He left a mess of dye in the bathroom, smears on the mirror and skylight, the toilet handle, the old scraggly towels.

Though he diligently re-dyed his white streak, he did not bathe often, or brush his teeth. He had a vial of cologne, in the shape of a muscular male torso, which he sprayed on his armpits and crotch twice per day.

He had a number of silver rings on his fingers, which he never took off, and the skin around them had turned green.

There was a hole in one of the walls that Pax had made one night. He denied that he was angry when he did it and that it was an art project, like his used-toilet-roll collage in the bathroom, a brown honeycomb-like structure stuck to the wall with tape.

Angelo had a projector. He used to lie in bed, projecting silent films onto the wall until Alexander complained about the light and motion. He watched them in the bathroom, sitting in the bathtub smoking hash from a pipe, or on the toilet, shitting while eating salty peanuts and drinking gin.

Late in the night, the others could hear him throwing up after too much gin. There were always specks of vomit in the toilet the next day, which none of them cleaned. They hardened, along with specks of faeces, the water never powerful enough to reach it.

They liked to go dancing, even on weekday evenings, to a club called Paradise Night. Pax had a blue button-down shirt with a pattern of black zigzags and white Corinthian columns which he liked to wear out. He put pomade in his hair and extra cologne. Alexander never drank, or took any drugs, but he danced like a maniac, especially when Devo came on. By the end of the night, Pax was always so drunk they had to stop him from beating up girls he thought were ugly. On the way home they stopped for food at a diner, Angelo and Pax gorging themselves on hot dogs, French fries, cheeseburgers. Alexander only had a glass of water with ice, cold milk, or maybe a ginger ale, and endless cigarettes.

They had one telephone they used only for hacking games. It could call anywhere in the world at no cost. Alexander also figured out a way to call everyone in the city simultaneously. Angelo was the speaker, and would say something like, 'We're out of potatoes, we're all out of potatoes,' before hanging up. They called foreign politicians, famous actors, all sorts of people in the same manner. Angelo had a long list of people to call that he kept adding to. A secretary at the Intl Computer Company who bothered him, an academic whose work on the nineteenth century he disagreed with, an aging actress with a young husband.

On the weekends, the three of them took a train or bus out of the city into the mountains and forests for a hike. Angelo was reckless. He brought along a small metal first aid kit and relished cleaning and dressing his wounds. He liked to stick his used bandages, bloodied side up, all over the wall near his bed. Along with his bandage collection, there was a cast of his lower arm from when he'd broken the bone. The three of them had drawn ancient-looking designs all over it with markers. They had once hired a cleaner, but she took Angelo's bandage collection off his wall and threw them out. They never hired a cleaner again and Angelo soon built up a new collection.

Pax always brought a heavy book on their hikes, which he didn't read once, not even on the train ride home.

Because Pax had horrible breath, if he forgot his water bottle on one of their hikes, the others hated to lend him theirs, even when he was coughing and gasping with thirst. Alexander got into the habit of bringing two water bottles, along with a pickaxe and rope. They all wore brown hiking boots with red laces and practical, waterproof parkas.

If they didn't go for a hike on the weekend, they went to a museum to look at Greek and Roman art, then to their favourite occult shop which sold books and interesting objects. They walked to the bookshop from the museum, their arms linked, their wool scarves following in the wind, Alexander never in the middle so he could hold a cigarette with his empty hand, Angelo reciting a string of code in a poet voice:

'01011001 01101111 01110101

01100011 01100001 01101101 01100101

01100100 01100101 01110100 01100101 01110010

01101101 01101001 01101110 01100101 01100100

01100010 01100101 01100011 01100001 01110101

01110011 01100101

01001001 01110111 01100001 01110011

01101100 01100001 01110010 01100111 01100101

01100010 01100101 01100011 01100001 01110101

01110011 01100101

01001001 01110111 01100001 01110011

01110010 01101111 01100001 01110010 01101001

01101110 01100111'

Alexander liked to get books on t'ai chi, Buddhism and ancient Greek rituals, and Angelo books on witchcraft, especially ones with illustrations and photos of naked, goat-headed people lying on pentagrams drawn on floors.

Pax bought a new ring with a yin and yang symbol on it, Angelo some tarot cards. Alexander bought a bag of rainbow-coloured chakra stones, which he later placed across his body from hips to head while naked in a waterless bath, and a book called *The Coiled Serpent: A philosophy of conservation and transmutation of reproductive energy* by Cornelius Johannes Van Vliet. He found the book in the discount box outside the occult shop. It was a secondhand copy, and inside was a yellowed scrap of newspaper with a review of the book, the only review to exist. The cover was green and white, depicting a topless, big-breasted woman and a man entwined by a snake. Beneath the title was printed 'The Enigma of Sex'. Alexander bought it, though the other two had giggled at the cover.

They were surprised at Alexander buying a book on sex.

Alexander did not have a box of tissues or a tin of moisturiser by his bedside, and they had never known him to masturbate at all.

Of course he did, in public toilet cubicles, quickly and quietly, multiple times a day, feeling miserable and depleted afterwards.

The other two didn't know that he also slept with a woman, Rosie, a couple of times every week, as Rosie's boyfriend Gerald wouldn't sleep with her until they were married. She had long hair down to her thighs and lived in a dark ground-floor apartment full of fake flowers in an odd assortment of vases. As a hobby she played the classical flute, and Alexander was disgusted whenever she did, her mouth moving along the metal flute hole, breathing in and out. She always insisted on playing a few pieces by Vivaldi or Mozart before they went to bed to put herself into a romantic mood. When she was finished, she took her flute apart into three sections, spit falling out of the holes as she did so, and put it in a blue-velvet-lined case.

He liked to spit in her asshole as she lay, crouched on her knees naked on the bed, holding her butt cheeks open. She begged him to stay the night but he never did. He always needed to make a bowel movement after sex and only liked to do it at home.

Alexander also had an unofficial agreement to meet a girl in a cinema every Sunday afternoon. They sat near the back and masturbated each other. They didn't greet each other in the cinema lobby, and Alexander wasn't exactly sure what she looked like because they only touched in the dark and he removed his glasses, which made him almost blind. The films were just colourful blurs. It didn't matter what film was playing since he couldn't remember any of them, and the girl could have been twenty or forty, he did not know.

The evening of the day Alexander bought *The Coiled Serpent*, Pax had a girl over that he had met through a newspaper ad. Pax and the girl came home drunk. Sometime in the night she said, 'I want to go home and sleep in my own bed, Pax.'

'No, stay the night, stay the night,' he said and pulled her back onto the bed, putting her in a headlock. She whimpered all night, but the others did not intervene.

She slid out, smelling of sweat and tired-eyed, first thing in the morning, without even putting her stockings on, though it was cold outside.

Angelo never had girlfriends or regulars, he only hired sex workers.

'All the other men must be so old, ugly and rich,' he liked to say to them between thrusts. 'They must make you feel so sad and dirty.'

That night, Angelo had masturbated, listening and seeing the shadows of Pax and the girl behind the paper screen. Alexander was up all night, reading *The Coiled Serpent* in bed with a torch.

Any kind of excitement or stimulation of the organs of generation is a disruptive waste of energy.

The next day Alexander wrote a curt letter to the musician saying he could not see her anymore. But instead of sending it, he just ripped it up and threw it in the rubbish. There was no reason to contact her at all to tell her he didn't want to see her again. He did not stop in one of his usual station toilet cubicles on the way to work. *The Coiled Serpent* had told him that if he retained his semen, did not waste it on sex, he could harness the energy and send it to his brain, becoming more productive, more spiritual, immortal even. *Gonads, throat, brain.* He was wasting energy from each on sex. There was a coiled serpent at the base of his spine which he needed to control instead of letting it control him.

Sexual purification is a requisite for the harmoniously balanced physical, moral, mental and spiritual development of the race.

Whenever he felt an erection, or visualised the musician's anus, he went into the bathroom and poured ice-cold water on his penis and testicles.

He used Pax's computer at home, building program after program at night, rarely sleeping. Pax told him to build another one and said all of Alexander's cigarette smoke would ruin the hardware.

The musician sent him desperate letters on perfumed sheets of blue paper which he threw in the rubbish unopened, and she would often shout, 'Yoo-hoo!' from the street up to their windows.

Soon, Alexander was promoted, with a massive increase in salary, but he did not make any purchases or move into an apartment on his own. He put his extra money between the pages of his copy of *The Golden Bough*. The other two wanted to know what his secret was and he gave them *The Coiled Serpent* to read. They vowed to keep their semen. 'Your seed is pure energy,'

Alexander told them. They needed to start meditating with him, and also stop drinking alcohol, eating bad food, start working out. Angelo threw his bottle of gin out of the window.

The three planned to leave the Intl Computer Company and start their own computer company. They bought resistors, capacitors, circuit boards that looked like cities viewed from an airplane, soldering irons and microchips, black, green and red wires, monitors, all from an electronics shop called Surplus Parts Galore, and started to build a new supercomputer. They used old leather suitcases, scraps of metal and even an old dead fridge they found by the communal bins to enclose it. It grew and grew, taking up more of the attic flat. It hummed all day and night and became so full of dust that they had to buy feather dusters and a small hoover. They covered the holes in the ceiling with plastic bags so the computer would not get wet.

The three of them were curious about Cornelius Johannes Van Vliet. They didn't know if he was dead or alive, but they wanted to name their computer company Serpent Inc. in his honour.

Asking around in occult shops and spiritual clubs, they heard that Cornelius Van Vliet was 3 feet tall, wore a large pendant over his turtleneck (though the person telling them couldn't remember what was on the pendant – a pentagram, a snake, a Greek letter or something else obscure and unknown) and a long, flowing cape which dragged along the street behind him. Elsewhere, they heard that he had been a friend of Aleister Crowley; or that he was in fact 7 feet tall, youthful and spent a lot of time in museums, seriously brooding over art, or in sex clubs, watching orgies but not participating – a calm observer in a black turtleneck with a book of Schopenhauer under his arm; that he had the biggest penis in the world though it was never erect; that he collected taxidermy snakes and mystical Asian statues.

Based on these rumours, the three of them went to an antique shop and pooled their money to purchase a taxidermy snake in a glass Victorian box surrounded by plastic plants. They put it on top of the computer, where it sometimes vibrated.

Alexander went to various public libraries to research (none of the libraries had copies of *The Coiled Serpent*) until he found a reel of microfilm of an old newspaper with Cornelius's death announcement.

Our friend and yours,
   Mr C. J. Van Vliet
   Peacefully passed on to the next stage of Existence at Sunset, 17 September 1964. Let all who follow the LIGHTED WAYS work in unison to bring more light into the life of their fellow creatures. The rapture of eternal consciousness awaits you at the end of the path.

He had the librarians make a paper copy of the microfilm and brought it home to show Angelo and Pax.

'It doesn't say he died, it just says he passed on to the next stage of existence,' said Angelo.

Angelo continued to bring home sex workers, but practised retention – having sex but not letting his semen out. 'I feel the semen travel up my spine to my brain instead, like I am impregnating my mind, not a girl,' he said. Pax said he wanted no more women in the house, so Angelo would just have to masturbate or go elsewhere. They could hear him masturbating in the bathroom, stopping himself from coming. He would inhale deeply, moan and swear.

Angelo and Pax threw out all of their pornography books and films, even Alexander's copy of *The Story of Art*, which had images of naked female statues and paintings, and under the desperate circumstances might excite them. Alexander said they would all get to the point where they could test themselves by going to nightclubs and museums again, but it would take a while – months, probably – before they could master observing the way Cornelius Van Vliet had been said to do.

Unknown to the others, Angelo visited brothels where he paid to spoon and cuddle sex workers. He touched their heads, their feet, laid his head on their arms.

Finding one of Pax's old dating newspapers stuffed behind the toilet, he contacted a woman named Hilda with bleach-blonde spiky hair who described herself in the ad as 'a feminist poet and a witch'. He let himself come every three times he was with her. He liked to do it on her face, then lick it off and swallow it, thinking it didn't count as ejaculation if he put it back into his body. If he came inside a condom, he poured the contents straight into his mouth in the bathroom after taking it off himself. Angelo stole little wiccan trinkets from Hilda: crystals, oddly shaped candles, charm necklaces, unlabelled packets of herbs which smelled interesting, and gave them to Pax and Alexander as presents. He didn't think either of them noticed he wasn't retaining as purely as they were.

Pax, Alexander and Angelo worked out together when they were not programming at home. They purchased more dumbbells and an old rusty kettlebell. The apartment was so hot from the growing computer that Pax started to work out naked, Angelo in his blue and purple swimming shorts, but Alexander refused to take off his jeans, shirt or hat, sweat pouring down from it onto his face in rivers. The hat smelled like old sweat. He bought a black baseball cap to wear instead and threw out his smelly beanie hat. They all quit the Intl Computer Company and when not working out or working on the computer, they meditated, sitting cross-legged in a row on the floor, the only sounds in the apartment their breathing and the computer hum, in unison.

They bulked up. Their skin glowed with vigour. They looked like Greek statues of athletes; then, after working out more, bags stuffed to the brim with rocks and taut string. They had to buy new clothes, extra-large army surplus ware.

They continued to work on the computer. It grew and grew and could do more things. It had multiple monitors, black, green and bulging. Pax said it looked like the mythical monster Argus Panoptes. Their electricity bill was enormous: they went and bought battery power generators. There were multicoloured wires spreading across their floor like liquorice and candy laces, which they had to carefully step over. In an excited state, Angelo wrote, 'This Machine is as Big as our Cocks' on one metal side of the computer with a Sharpie. They printed out long swathes of paper with information on it, which they stacked in the bathtub and the oven.

They had to rearrange their sparse furniture in order to accommodate the growing computer and their growing bodies.

Alexander felt his heartbeat become rapid but he didn't tell the others. Even when he lay in bed at night, reading and smoking, his heart beat faster and faster, pounding in his brain. He had a hot feeling in his lower stomach and groin. During the few hours that he slept, he had nightmares about shitting live snakes. Feeling a warm breeze from one of the computer fans, he decided that what they really ought to be doing was making the computer smaller and smaller, as small as possible, like a flea, but even more powerful than it was now.

The next day, as Alexander lifted the kettlebell during their workout, he exploded.

Angelo and Pax removed the largest chunks of Alexander, his head, upper torso and feet, and put them in bin bags, but they didn't bother with all the smaller bits. There was hair and fat and blood stuck to the walls and floors, and bits of bone and hair had gone through the vents of the computer. There was an eye that had rolled under Pax's bed and shrivelled up. They took the bin bag with his head to a graveyard, as his head was so noble and handsome they didn't want to just throw it out. They removed his black baseball cap; his blond hair beautiful and soft. There was a large hole in the back of his head, through which they could see loosened bits of brain, like ramen packet noodles softened in a boiling pot of water. They buried the head under the magnificent grave of someone who had been dead for a long time.

The computer gave off a smell of boiled pork, and sometimes of singed hair, from the minuscule bits of Alexander still stuck to its warm surface. Angelo and Pax continued to work on it. They moved all of Alexander's things, along with his bed, into the bathroom, to make more space for the computer. When Angelo went to see

Hilda next, she picked a bit of scab and blond hair off his head and got angry because she thought it belonged to another girl. He lied and said it did, and she threw some sort of sharp metal wiccan tool at his forehead where it broke the skin. At home, he put a bandage over it, but didn't bother about the blood which had dribbled down his cheek and was starting to flake like cheap paint.

Pax was next. It happened when he was doing a squat. The dumbbell he had been using got covered in guts, blood, phlegm, shit. The explosion was so intense there weren't any recognisable chunks of Pax. He covered the computer like a sauce.

Angelo continued his workout instead of stopping to clean up, even as the apartment became increasingly hot, thick with the smell of burning meat. There was Pax's pulp all over Angelo's face, and soon tears too. He couldn't see anything clearly but he didn't wipe his eyes, just continued to lift the weights up and down. He felt his muscles bulge.

01001000 01100101

01101101 01110101 01110011 01110100

01110101 01101110 01101100 01101111 01101111 01110011 01100101

01110100 01101000 01100101

01100011 01101111 01101001 01101100 01110011

01100010 01100101 01100110 01101111 01110010 01100101

01110100 01101000 01100101
01101101 01101111 01101110 01110011 01110100
01100101 01110010
01100011 01110010 01110101 01110011 01101000
01100101 01110011
01101000 01101001 01101101

The Meat Eater

I was thirty-four years old, overweight, ugly and had a high IQ. I dropped out of my PhD on the feminist modernist poet H.D. and had stopped eating all food except for meat and fish. It has improved all my health problems, including acne, eczema, tremors and epileptic seizures that once left me bedridden for days. I have lost a lot of weight, but this has just made me a different sort of ugly. My nose looks bigger and my eyeballs stick out.

When I dropped out of my PhD, one of my professors told me I could stay in their unused basement apartment indefinitely.

My professor had lived in the apartment during his grad-school days and now just kept it for overspill of his collection of indigenous artefacts from Canada, South America and New Zealand, and his collection of Soviet art. The walls were covered in masks, and there was a Haida nation totem pole and a birch canoe in the main room, with paddles depicting crows. There were paintings of muscly, handsome men utilising machines, of Lenin addressing crowds, busts of Stalin, Marx and Mayakovsky. I fell in love with Mayakovsky's great, bald head, I looked up his name from the bust and discovered he was a poet. I took him down from his perch on a shelf and laid him down on the floor, face up. I sat on top of him, rubbing my pussy against his marble nose and brow. I did it so often he developed an off-white, green-tinged skin from my bodily fluids.

I didn't have a bed, just a pile of old clothes I didn't wear anymore which I slept on like a nest. I only liked to wear my green Maoist cap, my camouflage jacket, a white dress and a pair of black boots.

I ate steak, venison, ground beef, chicken, ribs, mackerel, lamb chops, salmon, tuna steak. My shopping basket and my fridge were full of beige, brown, red, silver, white. No sausages or bacon because they had added grains or sugar. My pee and sweat smelled like fried liver. I drank tons of water.

When I first started my meat diet I tried raw meat, which made me throw up for four hours, until my throat was hoarse and I couldn't tell what was my own blood and what was animal blood. I had waves of explosive diarrhoea and constipation, but now it's levelled out, and I shit like any carnivore animal does, densely and less frequently. I got worms, which looked like broken pieces of dental floss in my shit. My asshole itched all the time, but the worms made me feel less alone – like something was growing, procreating inside of me, so I just left them and didn't get any medication to kill them.

I found out that you get fewer nutrients, not more, from eating raw meat.

I did a full body workout every day – squats, push-ups, elbow planks, jumping jacks, punches – while listening to the Pet Shop Boys. I lifted weights, but nothing larger than 2 lbs because I didn't want muscly, masculine-looking arms. I also walked 8 km every morning. I didn't believe in running because it ruins your knees, and I liked to listen to my audiobook, a biography of Jian Qing, the wife of Mao, on my cassette player, while walking around the city. I got it from the library: eight cassettes in a large plastic package, with Jian Qing on the cover.

I discovered Jian Qing when the East Asian studies department of the university screened one of her Maoist opera ballets, before I dropped out. The next day I bought a green Maoist cap with a red star on it from a vintage shop.

She hung herself in jail using an accumulation of socks.

She once said, 'I am without heaven and a law unto myself,' which I wrote on a piece of paper and stuck to the wall, between the masks.

I also had dozens of pictures of Mayakovsky pasted between the masks and paintings. Some of the pictures I had photocopied from university library books or torn out. I thought he was the most handsome man ever to have lived. He was large, domineering, elegant. I had a bilingual edition of his poems, an old Soviet publication I stole from the library.

Mayakovsky was toothless, save for a few rancid brown stubs, and he impregnated multiple girls. When he met Lilya Brik, she got him a new set of teeth.

I have a fantasy list of procedures I would get done if I ever had money: nose job, brow softening, fillers, legs longer, butt and boob jobs since I lost both with my weight loss. I think my eyes are too close together, but moving eyes around seems too advanced for the medical establishment at this point in time. I would like plastic surgeons to smash my skull in, then rebuild it around my brain in a style of my choosing.

Men weren't like Mayakovsky anymore: now they liked superheroes and video games, they had Batman tattoos and Spider-Man figurines, they had flabby torsos from eating too many soy products, and they dressed like children.

The last man I had slept with had put on a pair of smelly fleece *Star Wars* pyjamas before we had sex. He was scrawny, except for his belly and breasts.

He didn't even like me: on our date he kept saying hello and whistling at attractive women who walked past us. He didn't like my looks and he wasn't interested in my personality. I was just a hole.

I dropped out of my PhD after attending a reading by a famous poet, organised by my department. She was a glamorous young woman and read out, in a disgusted voice, a poem that was a list of words men had called her on the street: 'hot bitch', 'sexy lady', 'whore', 'baby'.

I wished men would call me those names on the street, instead of barking like a dog at me or ignoring me altogether.

I walked out of the reading and dropped out at the end of that semester, finishing up the courses I was tutoring. I got a disciplinary for telling a student their work was shit, but I didn't care anymore.

I didn't want to spend my life writing essays on women like her and their fake problems.

I got fitter, my skin got clearer, but still men I was attracted to did not approach me. I continued to hang around campus a lot; my library card still worked, so I took out books on topics I was now interested in. There was a man I had seen around campus, he was very tall with a shaved head, and so reminded me of Mayakovsky. He was always with a different beautiful girl – young ones, with blue, pink or blonde hair. He never noticed me.

I saw him working out in a gym, and he always brought a book with him – Schopenhauer or Wittgenstein. He must have been a philosophy student. He often went to nightclubs popular with students and almost always left with a girl, though now and then he did not.

I ordered a gun from a catalogue I found at an anarchist bookshop. The catalogue also sold vegan milk alternatives and nuts in bulk, ingredients for making bombs, badges and kerchiefs with slogans on them.

The gun came inside a plastic doll in a parcel. The stomach of the doll had been sawed open then glued shut again. The gun was wrapped in bubble wrap. It was quite small. The bullets weren't in the gun, but loose inside the doll's body and I had to shake them out.

The time I caught him alone, he was wearing a green camouflage winter coat and coming out of the university library as it was closing. It was exam season so he was partying less and less often in the company of other girls.

I took him by gunpoint back to my apartment. He was so tall and big he had to hunch to go through my door.

I thought I should give him the gun, hoping that maybe he would point it at me and rape me and shoot me, but there was the horrible possibility that he would just leave if he had it, that there was nothing else keeping him in my apartment but the gun.

He did not show any signs of attraction towards me, and made no moves to seduce me. He did not even notice my Mayakovsky books or pictures of Mayakovsky on the wall. He showed a slight interest in some of the tribal masks, but they had nothing to do with me. I had purchased regular refreshments for him: beer, vodka, pretzels, apples. I offered them to him but he said no. He smoked cigarettes until he ran out – I hadn't thought to buy him cigarettes though I had seen him smoking many times. I told him I was a carnivore but he didn't show any interest in that statement.

I kept looking at his crotch. He was crouched, smoking. There was no sign of hardness, and I realised too late that I could have bought a metal cock ring which would force him into an erection. I wasn't going to be able to have sex with him; he wouldn't have sex with me. I shot him in the chest.

I dragged his body over to the canoe and pushed it in by tipping the canoe over, though the blood stained the birch sides of it, which wouldn't please my former professor. His mouth was agape and filled with blood. I put his hand on his chest, like the famous suicide photo of Mayakovsky.

I found a lighter and his student ID in his pocket. He was Polish, and his name was Bartek Miklasinski.

I cut out chunks of his lower torso, since it was already open from the bullets, and ate pieces raw, with my hands. It seemed too normal for me to fry him in a frying pan or roast pieces of him with salt in the oven.

The next morning, his mouth smelled. He would start to rot soon. The wisest thing for me to do would've been to cut him up, wrap the pieces in plastic and stick them in the fridge, and generally treat him like meat from then on, but I wanted to keep him as a boyfriend too, which he would no longer be if cut up into pieces. I gave up after cutting off one of his feet, which I cradled and kissed before putting it back by his ankle, where I had sawn it off. A man can still live a good life, missing one foot.

I did eat the meat I already had in the fridge, to make room, but even when my fridge was empty, I didn't fill it with him.

I slept in the other room, but I had fantasies that he woke up and came into my room and fucked me, or even just slept beside me. Sometimes I heard sounds in the other room and waited, in anticipation, before falling asleep. I had cosy dreams about him. In one we lived in a trailer and had a baby I had lots of photos of, though I couldn't find the baby and I was too distracted by a series of colourful and intricate mushrooms growing out of my feet. He drove a hearse, not as a job, but had bought the hearse secondhand – it still had an old coffin in it we hadn't opened or taken out. I would wake up from these dreams to hear creaks from the living room, though he never left the canoe. The masks and busts sometimes seemed to have shifted around the room, or their eyes and mouths had changed. The Marx bust grinned.

I put on his camouflage coat and my Maoist hat and went out and bought a ton of philosophy books for him from the university bookshop. I hoped girls he had slept with saw me in his coat and realised I was his girlfriend now. There was blood from when I'd shot him dribbled on the front of the coat, but no one seemed to notice. I bought cigarettes, too – his brand, Marlboro Gold.

I put the books in the living room for him to read, and smoked one of his cigarettes.

The lighter was still in the pocket of his jeans. I took off his Doc Martens and his socks. His feet were all swollen and deformed from death. I put them in my mouth and sucked but didn't bite them. I had pulled his shirt down again, covering the part of his torso that I'd eaten, but I dipped my hand in the gunshot wound, covering it with thick blood.

Between the masks on the wall I fingerpainted different body parts and organs: kidneys, toes, eyes, genitals. I captured my man's ears, hands and shaved head while they were still decipherable.

White Asparagus

I have five rooms, each with a different pattern of wall-paper that seems unfitting, as if the rooms once served a different purpose. The living room has nursery paper with a design of ducks in ribbon hats pushing prams, and there are red racing cars in the kitchen. The bathroom is dark and complex, a rich forest full of parrots and tigers almost entirely obscured by mould. I cannot open the window as it has been covered by a wallpaper patterned with daisies. Only a faint light shines through, although whether this is from the sun or a lamp, I don't know. There are small brownish-grey mushrooms growing out of the floor and walls.

My bedroom has a cheery design of tiny blue people carrying milk pails – more suitable to a kitchen, perhaps. The bedroom would be large if it wasn't filled with wooden wardrobes, some of which are locked. It is a project of mine to work on opening them, and perhaps dismantling them altogether.

I have quite a lot of clothes – jumpers, socks, trousers, wool stockings, dresses, wire and lace bras. I have to hand-wash them in the kitchen sink, and they shrink every time. Someday they will become too small for me and I will have to cut them up and sew them into something bigger.

My rooms are part of a larger structure; my main door leads onto a hallway, which I can see through the keyhole.

Each week I am given a parcel of food which changes seasonally. I am always delighted when there is white asparagus, grapes or apricots. Yet every week there is jam, tinned fish, bouillon powder or cubes, crackers, cans of grape and orange soda, which I do not like and stack in the kitchen cupboard, various teas in small Chinese tins, wine gums, hot chocolate powder, a green cabbage, a container of snails.

I've started growing plants from a few of the fresh vegetables by putting their scraps in jam jars filled with water. After a few weeks thin white roots, like noodles, appear. I have a whole room filled with mulch made from my food waste. I keep it in the room that also contains a long rubber hose I do not know the purpose of. I do not know the wallpaper pattern of that room as there is no light or window.

There are a few windows in my rooms. Two are stained glass, so rich, colourful and detailed that nothing can be discerned about what is on the other side. They look too beautiful to break, and there is metal netting, as one sees in very old cathedrals to protect the glass. On bright days the netting looks like a thick spider's web that is part of the depicted scene, of the stained-glass world where everyone has to constantly brush past spider's webs like curtains.

The rest of the windows are, like the bathroom, covered with pictures – chocolate-box-like scenes of forests and city streets glued directly to the glass. Another one of my projects is to scrape away at them using a coin I have, as money has no other use to me.

In the living room, besides a fireplace and several nice still-life paintings, I have an ancestral head on a plaque. It doesn't speak, only moaning now and then and making painful, weary facial expressions. I feed it thin soup and jam. I don't know where it all goes besides the bits that dribble down its chin, but it always takes pleasure in food. Its hair is coarse and sparse, its pallor very similar to the bathroom mushrooms. The ancestor on a plaque is nailed to the wall, but as the wallpaper is rotting, it became too weak to hold them anymore and the ancestor fell off. The ancestor's nose became bruised and scabbed for some time after, but it healed eventually. Not wholly, but well enough. They now sit on the mantelpiece, and enjoy the warmth of the fire, but moan silently when it is too much.

There was one terrible day when I became curious about one of the cupboards in the hall and opened it.

Inside was a tiny old man sitting in a tiny striped armchair. He held a small porcelain lidded pot with Greek patterns and he was fiddling with it, taking off the lid and putting it back on. Looking at the designs, he hardly noticed me.

The floor was littered with very old, rotting apple cores and the man smelled. I shut the door.

For months afterwards I felt an uncomfortable lurch when I walked past it and I didn't know if I should open it again, but after a while the feeling went away.

I comfort myself with the thought that perhaps the cupboard has a little door I haven't seen, leading to whole hidden rooms, and the man gets his own food parcels delivered. Or that he is so long dead by now that there is no point in me looking.

Not long after that, I regained a sense of harmony and stoicism when, along with my usual parcel of food, another person arrived: a short young man with a beard and long hair, wearing a baggy pinstripe suit whose sleeves were too long for him. He eyed the parcel of food with curiosity and hunger, and without asking, took a banana from it and ate it. He stuffed the peel in his jacket pocket afterwards.

I moved all my bedroom things – my jumpers, my books – into the living room, as I did not trust the other person with the ancestor; perhaps they would touch it or had knives or scissors and would cut it. I thought I could have more claim on the rest of the rooms if I gave him the largest one, and, without me needing to tell him, the other person took possession of the bedroom.

He wanders the halls and sits in the kitchen and bathroom for long periods of time.

I go to the kitchen to make myself tea and discover it is full of smoke. The other person has taken all the food from the parcel, put it into a pot and cooked it to a burnt sludge. They have thrown the tins and peelings all over the floor.

I take clippings from all of my plants and turn them into a thin soup with the addition of salt from a container in the kitchen that the other person has not yet found. The ancestor eats it obligingly, their eyes rolling around in their head.

The next morning all the mushrooms are gone from the bathroom – he has eaten them. The toilet is also clogged, his excrement larger than a whole cabbage. I have to chop it up with a spoon to make it go down, and pointedly leave the spoon unwashed beside the toilet for future use.

He wanders the halls, making odd mewing and whimpering sounds, sometimes stopping to gaze at me and the ancestor, but we make no signs of distress or hunger for him to see. I calmly read out loud from my book of ferns. I have a bunch of books, some I have brought with me and some I found in the apartment. My favourites are a

Rupert Bear book, a collection of old poems, a book on fern cultivation, a cookbook that only refers to meat – which I was not given in my parcels but I am interested in nonetheless as it is full of diagrams. I am particularly worried about the new person finding this, especially in a hungry mood. The ancestor looks lamblike, and there is one diagram of a cow's head that rather reminds me of myself.

He discovers my stacks of grape and orange fizzy soda which I have not got desperate enough to drink yet. He drinks one can after another until he throws up, then goes back to his hungry mewing when he recovers. There are foamy piles of purple and orange spittle everywhere.

As I know the precise time the parcel arrives each week, I wait by the door for it and grab three quarters of the food. I am particularly fond of a dish I call 'Cabbage in the Garden', where I boil the snails and cabbage together, and of course I need jam for the ancestor, but I leave a large turnip, a tin of fish and a lot of the tea for the other person.

He carries the turnip around under his arm importantly for a few days, and eats the tea straight from the tin, the leaves stuck between his teeth. He stops to ask me what to do with the turnip as I am leaving the bathroom, which makes me realise he has been carrying it around, hoping I would notice. I say it is to be eaten raw, as I do not want him taking up too much time in the kitchen.

This cures his constipation at least, and the toilet is not as clogged as previously, though he cried plenty as he went.

He sings a lot to himself, and once passing the bedroom, where the door was open, I caught him moaning and touching himself as he rubbed one of the tiny blue milkmaids on the wallpaper with the index finger of his other hand.

It occurs to me, at night as I lie awake on the fainting chair, that the old man in the cupboard, and perhaps even my ancestor, have diminished themselves since I moved in and I do not want to do the same to myself. It takes me a few days to figure out which animal he resembles in my meat cookbook, and that I should dispose of him this way.

There are no knives in the house, only forks and spoons, and I make a bad attempt to kill him by stabbing him in the cheek with a fork in the kitchen. He hides in his room whimpering afterwards, and I can hear him desperately trying to unlock the wardrobes, as if they are a way out.

It occurs to me that the food tins are very sharp, I cut myself on a lid once after opening it, and these I can use as thin knives.

A few days later, I see him emerge from his room to go to the kitchen to find food. The fork is still in place on his cheek, the skin swollen and red around it. He did not think to pull the fork out, and he can't chew any food. All he can manage is a can of grape soda, crying as he drinks it, the fork moving up and down as he swallows.

I ignore his movements and cries until they all stop, and I find him in the bedroom, his face all disfigured and green. I pull the fork out and wash it well.

Following my cookbook and with the help of my tin lids, I turn him into ribs, sausages and pâtés – a long, smelly and arduous process. But the results look very presentable, especially with a bit of garnish from a carrot plant, but I do not want to eat them and do not believe the ancestor can digest them either. I dispose of the various dishes in the room with the mulch and the hose, and clean the crockery I have used.

The Apartment

This is the story of six residents of the same apartment and how they all died.

A young man took over a nook in the stairwell directly outside the apartment. He moved a children's wooden bed frame with foxes on it and lay there, the bed surrounded by plastic bags full of food and toothbrushes and stuffed toys in the shape of hedgehogs and little girls.

One day, he was gone. All of his possessions had disappeared too, and there were pink puddles of antiseptic spray where his bed had been. No one in the apartment mentioned it to one another, and it is not talked about or included as a number in one of the six deaths!

The landlord rented the apartment room by room, with access to the shared bathroom, kitchen and large living room. Knowing how large the living room was, and how it could be used for party-balls even, the landlord divided two corners of it into more bedrooms using screen dividers, glass doors and Persian carpets that he used as ceilings. These Mongolian-like tents were rented out for the same price as the other bedrooms. In addition, he put a broken grand piano in the centre of the living room. It was enormous and unplayable: the two or three keys left were soft slivers of wood.

The current residents sold this grand piano. When the landlord came to do an inspection, they gathered together their suitcases and other contingent objects and vaguely formed them into the shape of a piano under several shawls and blankets. The landlord, glancing and busy, did not look underneath.

Luba, a resident of bedroom 1, had the most blankets to contribute to hiding the sale of the piano. Her bedroom was a mess of cloth: curtains, stained bedspreads, scarves, pillowcases, skirts, handkerchiefs like colourful mounds of tripe. She could not resist an interesting pattern. She intended to turn bedspreads into scarves, scarves into handkerchiefs, curtains into tablecloths, scraps into rag rugs, using a compact sewing kit she bought at a Chinese shop: a tiny pair of scissors, three colours of thread, six needles and two pins with pink tips, a silk pin ball with sweet Chinese babies on it, but this she lost under all the piles of cloth. A hunt through the piles for the kit led to her discovering crevices of cloth filled with tiny white maggots. Too afraid her roommates would see if she disposed of them in the kitchen or bathroom, she stuffed the maggoty fabric clots in bin bags which she took out at night and put in public bins.

Her walls were covered in postcards of cats; her favourite one was made with gold and silver foil. The landlord forbade animals, though there were rats and cockroaches and a giant reclining taxidermy tiger who was mouldy and full of holes. Bence, who lived in bedroom 3, removed the teeth, eyes and nails from the tiger and had them made into jewellery: a tooth earring, an eyeball ring, a nail bracelet. They were made with cheap metal which left green and grey stains on his skin.

Luba was in love with Bence. Bence was enormous, with a shaved head the back of which was flat, and black, rotting teeth.

Bence had a girlfriend who wore a fur coat made from cats bought from a lowly but famous fur shop which killed stray cats and dogs, ferrets, even rats, and turned them into clothing. Her name was Agne and she studied philosophy at the state university. She wore wristwatches around both her ankles, and sometimes a beaded purse on her head upside down as a hat, as her head was so narrow. Her face was very long, with protruding eyes, as if a fish's entire body had been stuck through the neck of her coat. She loved to eat seafood, especially anchovies. Bence did not understand. To him, they were simply grey strips of salt in beautiful tins. Bence spent all his money on seafood, in jars and tins, and sometimes fresh, for his girlfriend. He fried prawns which looked like little men with their whiskers, how strange! He bought a lobster which he boiled in the kitchen, then brought to bed where Agne was waiting. He didn't carry it on a plate, just in his arms like a baby to impress her, even though it was hot and steaming and Bence winced. They discarded the shells, claws and antennae around his room like bits of carnival costume. They rotted and smelled.

Luba had wanted Bence's room badly: it had once been a nursery and had wallpaper of little boys wearing ushankas and pretty girls with braids. Bence had drawn dirty things on all of them using charcoal.

Luba stole a blackened toothbrush from the communal bathroom which she thought must belong to Bence because of his horrible teeth, and used it to masturbate in her room. He didn't notice it was gone and didn't buy a new toothbrush either.

Bence and Agne took a silver powdered drug together which they ate from the scrunched-up red tissue it was sold in.

His girlfriend claimed to see and talk with all sorts of dead intellectuals when she was high – Theodor Adorno, Emma Goldman, Tolstoy, Susan Sontag – but could never remember afterwards what they'd told her. Bence tried to write it all down while it was happening, but when he looked at his notebook later it was full of tiny drawings of hands and feet, and that was it.

In the third room lived a religious studies student, Taras. He was thin, with a blond mullet and a silver chain around his neck, and wore brown leather sandals with grey socks. He told everyone else at the apartment that old women at his church often collapsed speaking in tongues.

He rarely used the communal kitchen, as he had a kettle and a hotplate in his room. The hotplate was covered in bits of burnt scrambled egg, but otherwise his room was very sparse and clean. There were two icons on his wall, each with a group of obscure and bearded saints.

He brought his cup and plate to be washed in the kitchen once per day. He ate the rest of his meals in the university canteen.

The kitchen was filled with old rusty appliances, more than any one family could use – pokers, graters, mills, rolling pins, cookie-cutters, jelly moulds, eggbeaters, casserole dishes, mallets, mushers, roasting tins, something resembling a miniature metal barrel organ with a rubber handle, funnels, tins that said 'Bread', 'Coffee', 'Flour' on them but contained only sticky grey dust.

The iron oven had seven compartments, in rectangular shapes of varying lengths and widths. There were two large hobs and the handles were porcelain. It heated unpredictably, so that sometimes food was burnt and sometimes it was still raw after hours. All the residents just used the hobs, big black circles like dirty scratched records, or ate things cold.

Antione, who lived in one of the tents, decided to use the oven. He bought some sausages which cooked into little burnt black wires. Though he couldn't eat them, he was satisfied by the process, that he had done something significant by feeding meat to the oven, by observing the force of its heat. He thought of the ancients who used to make meat sacrifices to the gods.

In the following days, he bought whatever meat was cheapest, and carried it home in large plastic sacks. He stuffed it in odd configurations into casserole dishes – a lamb's head surrounded by pig's feet, layers of bones, tripe and chicken's feet, which he cooked until the kitchen was filled with smoke and the meat was turned to ashes. When the other members of the apartment complained, he shrugged and said he was learning to cook. He was a young man away from his mother, what did they expect?

The second tent was occupied by Marian, a social-ist who did a lot of unpaid door-to-door campaigning, wearing a fedora hat and a jacket covered in various political badges. He was a vegetarian and his tent was surrounded by various jars of beans soaking in water until they became edible, pickled beets and slimy mush-rooms. He had a dreadful pallor and a pot belly.

Bence took Agne out to dinner at a riverside seafood restaurant. The chairs and tables were outdoors. They were given no menu, but a young man came around with a large wooden board with various fish nailed to it, the scaly remnants of older, eaten fish underneath them. His girlfriend chose an eel, Bence a wide red fish with big teeth. The young man disappeared into the kitchen and returned sometime later with the same fish roasted on plates, served with boiled sprouted potatoes and red wine from Hungary.

Later that night, very drunk, Bence dreamed the eel came out of Agne's orifices and slithered into his mouth. He woke up feeling sick.

He opened a door which he thought was the bathroom's and vomited on the floor then stumbled back to bed. It wasn't the bathroom, but Luba's bedroom. She awoke and saw his silhouette in her door.

In the morning she inspected his vomit: red stains and silver fish scales. She guessed he had planned to seduce her despite his girlfriend asleep in his own bedroom, but his being sick prevented it. She didn't wash away the vomit but watched it dry, a beautiful painting from his innards, until she realised it would prevent him from trying to seduce her again. She ate the sour, vinegar-tinged fish scales, picking them up with her fingertips, then scrubbed away the rest with bleach.

This meal, shared accidentally between Luba and Bence, was remembered by both for the rest of their short lives, as the government caused inflation to rise horribly not long after, and food became scarce and expensive.

Each citizen was given a small ration of half a loaf of strange, dense bread, which never went stale or mouldy, and three slices of pale pink spongy meat with white flecks in it. Marian did not eat his meat, but traded it for other foodstuffs. He traded two weeks' worth for a slab of tofu which ended up being a damp white sponge.

The landlord came in for another inspection, this time bringing a new friend who was an antiques dealer. They did not look at the 'piano' but the antiques dealer said he would send a piano specialist over to look at it, leaving all the residents of the apartment with acute dread.

They took what was left of the tiger, a few lamps from various bedrooms, a bag of dolls from one of the cupboards and the oven, which the antiques dealer said was made in Turkey in the nineteenth century. It was too big to take down the stairs or through the windows so they had it disassembled, leaving piles of black ash and rust everywhere. Bence said it didn't matter that they took the stove because there was no food anyway. The landlord, knowing this, did not replace it with a new stove. The Turkish oven was sold to a wealthy person abroad.

Everyone in the apartment thought resentfully of Antione with his piles of meat that he burnt to a crisp and how they should have stopped him and cured the meat and dried the bones to save for later.

Antione left little cuts of leather from his shoes and tiny bits of meat from his state ration under a large lamp in the living room outside his tent, but the pieces just rotted, or disappeared in the night, eaten by someone else. Bence called Antione an idiot for not eating them himself.

Bence's girlfriend moaned about having no fish to eat, so Bence went fishing in the city's main river every day. He only caught a small fish once, as the river was so overcrowded with new fishermen, with fishing rods made from walking sticks, threads from their wives' sewing baskets and tiny bits of their own flesh stuck to safety pins for bait, their hands and arms and noses covered in bandages. The lucky ones, with dandruff and callouses on their feet, did not have to endure any pain for bait.

In the apartment garden, Bence dug up slugs which he sliced thinly and put in old anchovy tins for Agne.

Together, everyone cut the apartment's leather couch into thin strips and boiled it using Taras's hotplate, an imitation tripe soup. All of them fantasised about the tiger the landlord had taken away: somewhere in its mildewing, embalmed body, there must have been a bone, maybe with a scraggly bit of ancient flesh clinging to it.

Bence sucked and gnawed on Agne's fur coat, and she slapped him for it.

Everyone shared one purple cabbage, each having a layer every day. Some of them used it as a wrap, filling it with nettles and leather, others boiled it and ate it as soup. Every morning Marian measured the cabbage to make sure no one took more than one leaf.

One miraculous day, Bence brought home a piglet wrapped in a wool blanket. He did not say how he got it, but he had a black eye and scratches all over his face. He said it was tempting for them all to eat it now but if they shared their scraps and nettles for months they would have ten times as much food in a few months. He entrusted it to Luba because she was a woman.

Luba made a nest in her bed for the piglet. Each of them sacrificed a portion of their bread to feed the piglet – they mixed the bread with water to make a paste. Luba loved the piglet, and could not think of the look of betrayal on the grown pig's face when it realised what she had loved and raised it for, as the older a pig became, the more intelligent it grew. She knew, if it even lived another month or two, she would name it Vladimir and it would be her son.

In the kitchen she threw it out of the window, in a bundle of blankets, pretending it was an accident. She screamed and made everyone else go down and retrieve the body. She didn't know that it was still slightly alive when Bence found it and that he crushed its chest with his boot and that this death was more painful, perhaps, than the death that awaited it as an adult. (None of them owned a gun or an axe, just the horrid cupboard of kitchen implements.)

They cut off the piglet's feet to make a jelly and preserved the rest of the body in it so that it appeared, footless, in a wobbly clear coffin.

When it was ready, and everyone stood around with a plate, even Luba, Bence cut into the piglet with the knife. Agne, who had been invited over for the special meal as long as she told no one else, screamed dramatically as he did so, as if she was the one being stabbed, then giggled when he was finished. She was maniacal with hunger.

Seeing Bence cut the pig, Luba wanted him to eat it whole then have sex with her and get her pregnant, so the piglet would be reborn from her and forgive her for throwing it from the window, but he served his girlfriend the first and largest piece of the pig. She watched the pig be chopped into pieces and distributed. Save the heart for me, thought Luba.

Even Marian was so hungry that he ate, though he only ate the gelatin, mixing it with bits of nettle.

As he ate his share, Antione thought how lovely it would be to watch the whole meal burn to a crisp in the old stove, how holy and miraculous it would be. This boiled meat was a double death, a smell of putrefaction.

Taras used this cheery occasion to announce that he had received a student visa to continue his studies in theology and he would be leaving in four days.

Everyone watched him enthusiastically chew his serving of pork. He was leaving for a place with plenty of food, and here he was, eating the small amount they had. He could survive four days on water!

Bence decided that in the night before he was supposed to leave, he would kill Taras and stick his own photo in Taras's passport. With his shaved head, and the cross necklace from his grandmother he always wore, he could pass as a devout theology student. He knew Taras would not indulge in food in his new country, but continue to eat scrambled eggs as he had here before inflation.

After the meal, Bence went to a photobooth in a metro station, and had his photo taken. He said the name 'Taras' as the camera flashed. He planned to beat Taras to death with a meat mallet from the kitchen as soon as he got home.

Later that day, Antione tied the lamp wire around his neck and choked himself to death. He left a note for the others: 'Please, if you come across some matches, burn my body.'

They buried him in the communal garden because they had no energy to carry him to the cemetery, and they also hoped his body would fertilise the nettles and other plants growing there that they had been subsisting on. Taras said a prayer over his grave.

The next day, Marian was beaten by fascists when leaving a socialist meeting about inflation. They kicked him to the ground and his hat fell off. When they were finished, he grabbed his hat and put it back on his now-bleeding head and ran home.

His hat was glued to his head with his own blood – it had become part of the scab of the wound. It was more painful than a bandage when he tried to peel it off, so he left it.

As he had planned, Bence did beat Taras to death with a mallet the night before he was supposed to leave, and left in his place with a packed bag. He posted a letter to his girlfriend saying he would send her a fish as soon as he could. He was intercepted at the airport: one of the photos he'd stuck over Taras had fallen off. There was no glue in the city – it had all been eaten – and he had stuck it on with some of the leftover gelatin from the pig. He was put in jail and swiftly executed, not just for the death of Taras, but also unjustly for that of Marian, who'd died in his bedroom tent from his head wound, the hat soaked through and crusted with blood. Luba, now alone in the apartment, gathered everyone's fabric belongings, their sheets (Bence's still smelling of rotten lobster), socks and shirts, and added to the pile in her room which stretched almost to the ceiling. She crawled into it, creating a dirty and dark tunnel, and with a tug on an old sleeve or stocking, buried herself.

Hoo Hoo

Hooo!

Woo!

Wooo!

Hoowoohoohoo!

There was a crack in the stone base of the monument, which we crawled into. A copper man on a beast above our heads. The woos were beginning. The creatures were waking up. It was dusk.

We couldn't fit all our stuff in the crack with us so we put it in front of the opening, hoping it wouldn't be torn open.

'We could've made it across just before evening,' Susan said, 'but we don't know what awaits us there. It's best to wait till early afternoon tomorrow when the creatures are deep in sleep.'

We quickly ate some Ovaltine powder – with our fingers to make less noise – then settled in, silent as we could be, for the night.

Unlike other nights, we knew where we wanted to go. Across the park was a red-brick building with very small windows. The small windows were why Susan wanted us to move there – the creatures couldn't get in through the windows. She had seen a photo of it in an old city guide. It was part of an old university, all the building fronts facing the round park where we hid in a monument. Some of the buildings had large, broken windows as big as small houses. They roosted in those buildings, there could be no doubt. The trees of the park were all scratched and covered in white splatters. The creatures made splatters and pellets.

In the morning, we found a pellet near us. It was still a bit wet, a large, dark grey cone.

Susan slit the pellet open with a knife, wearing gloves. The pellet was mostly made out of hair and fur, so they were easy to open. She wouldn't let me touch it, said it was full of poisons, but bits of fur ended up all over our clothes and in our mouths and eyes. She poked through it with a stick, pulling out a bit of string with a rock tied to the end of it, which she examined then threw aside. She found a shard of white porcelain with a blue design on it. 'I wonder if we'll find the whole piece of whatever it was in here,' she said.

She also found some coins, more porcelain, and a doll's arm, which she put in one of her plastic bags. The doll's arm we found had been swallowed because it looked like a child's arm, and the creatures couldn't tell the difference.

Some of our bags had been torn in the night, pecked through, but not much was taken as all of it was the inedible parts from pellets, well wrapped in plastic and string so they didn't look like anything edible.

The best way to get things, anything, was through the pellets of creatures. Everything they couldn't digest was thrown up in a grey or black pod. Things that could be digested: blood, flesh, semen, milk, phlegm, faeces, urine, paper, plants. Things that couldn't: hair, bone, gristle, nail, horn, porcelain, glass, metal, stones. When we found a place to spend the night, if there was space, Susan would light a fire and boil the things found in pellets in a kettle, to clean them, then wrap them up with a label. She wanted to establish a museum, and the building with small windows would be it.

The door of our building was shut, so Susan made me crawl through one of the windows: I was a small boy, she said. There was still glass, which she smashed with a stick. I wore enough layers to not get cut.

In the entrance hall were frames on the walls, full of small, egg-shaped photographs of women. Graduating class of 1972, 73 . . . 1992 . . . 1997. . . I noticed them before I noticed the door:

There was a board over the door.

'Let me in, are you okay?' asked Susan through the door. I had to rip off the board to let her in. She came in holding her frying pan high with one hand, and took my hand with the other.

The building was full of small rooms. Each had a fire-place and spare furniture – a bed frame, an armchair. We chose one not too high up, with its small window still intact. Susan made a fire using one of the framed grad-uation photos from downstairs, and boiled the things we'd found in the pellet that morning, as well as some Ovaltine, using the same water. Our foodstuffs were a jar of Ovaltine, paper boxes full of cocoa, baking soda, sugar, a gold and metal tin that said 'OATS' but now contained a brown powder not as tasty as the cocoa, and a green bottle with water in it. Susan kept the boxes and tins in her rucksack, with a few spoons held together with an elastic, and Maud's jumper.

She took Maud's jumper out of her rucksack to air it out. It was a pink jumper with little baubles on it that looked like nipples.

Maud was before my time, and all that remained of Maud was the jumper. The main thing Susan looked for in pellets was Maud. She planned to put Maud back together, I think – the bones, the teeth, the cloth, the gristle, the hair, the jumper, everything minus the blood, the flesh, the phlegm – and present her as the main display in her museum.

Susan took the doll's arm and bits of porcelain out of the pot and put the porcelain pieces together. 'Look,' she said. 'Fish.' There was a pattern of blue fish.

She always took pottery fragments when she found them in pellets. We stuck the larger fragments in our clothes using tape, glue, or string, to protect against the talons.

'But the noise!' I had said.

They can hear us regardless, she had replied. We packed the fragments so tightly in the linings of our coats that they didn't make much sound.

Once we found a whole suit of armour in a pellet. But we couldn't wear it to protect ourselves from talons, as it was much too small, even for me, though I was a little boy.

'Humans were smaller once and so were creatures,' Susan said.

Small enough to be swallowed whole.

We wore layers and layers of jumpers and coats to protect us from the talons. On top, I had a tartan coat and Susan had a dark green one.

We practised taking all the layers off.

You had to do it fast before the creature flew too high and dropped you.

Susan grabbed the back of my jumpers with her hands and held on tight while I tried to slip out of the top one as quickly as possible.

She never wore Maud's jumper; it didn't fit. Susan was very large. Her hair was black and cut short. We both wore two or three knitted caps most of the time.

The sharp things we found in pellets were terrifying. They made us feel defenceless, and the creatures invincible. Horns, claws, fangs, scissors, knives, wire, brooches. One time, there was a gold brooch shaped like a creature: 'They'd even eat a small version of themselves,' Susan had said. It had large jewel eyes. I hadn't ever seen a creature up close.

Susan believed she was one of the only persons left interested in cutting and collecting from pellets. She told me, 'There used to be a woman . . . she was all covered in jewels she collected from the pellets, said she would never have them otherwise, and so she was quite happy with the way things ended up. Well, I ended up finding all the jewels she wore and her bones in a pellet one day. Most people only care about potatoes, and cabbages, and being safe; they don't care about things, or what's gone.'

There were shops; the one we knew was open two hours per day. There were grates over the windows and doors and you had to ring a bell to get in. It was high-ceilinged but stuffy and smelly inside – the smell of potatoes, cabbages. They sold Ovaltine, vegetables, books and other papers, and gum – the smell of which was supposed to ward off creatures, but Susan knew it didn't as she often found it in pellets. Creatures didn't like to eat vegetables, unless they were desperate, so there were many, Susan told me. Susan did not like potatoes, but she did not mind potato flakes, she said. Sometimes you could buy potato in a tin all flaked and dry like oatmeal. It was in that shop that Susan bought a soft-covered book with photos of all the different buildings and decided upon the one to house her museum. It had once been a dormitory for female students, the book said. 'Look at all the tiny windows. A creature couldn't fly through one of those.'

Besides pellets, we once found a nest, large white eggs sitting in a pile of feathers, string, dead mice. I grabbed one of the mice and put it in my coat pocket.

One of the eggs moved. Susan gasped and covered my eyes with one of her hands, and pulled me backwards. 'I do not want you to see that,' she said.

And we found a food cache, I remember. Creatures made caches of food when they had more than they could eat. There were lots of mice, rats, a baby raccoon, a small child who didn't look right: its limbs were very thin, its head very long and large, and it had dark bruises under its bulbous eyelids and its phallus was purple. Looking at the mice made me feel hungry and I wanted to grab a few but Susan said no, not those ones – I'll catch you some myself, those ones you ought not to eat.

There was nothing we could take to eat – and just looking at it made Susan ill – but Susan grabbed all the pellets there and put them in a bin bag she kept for carrying them. It was no good slitting them near the cache.

Susan had her own caches of things that were too large to carry with us. She would pick them up later when we were settled. Dinosaur bones. An atlas. They were wrapped in plastic and buried in the ground, with some sort of marking.

The walls of the building, our future museum, were noisy: full of mice and rats.

'I should have known there would already be those hiding from the creatures here,' Susan sighed when we settled down to bed. 'We'll just have to live with them. I want to stay here.'

My stomach rumbled: I thought of eating them, the mice.

I found a dead one in our room, in the drawer of a chest that had been left. I stuffed it into my mouth and chewed quickly. I couldn't wait to boil it.

I usually liked to slice them open and eat all around the bones and fur.

'That's not healthful, eating solid things,' Susan muttered, seeing me eat it. 'Besides, the creatures can hear your crunches when you do.'

The mice and rats crawled around everywhere, all around our things; they weren't afraid. The next morning we looked through the building to plan out our museum.

Susan kept a notebook in which she labelled everything found in each pellet, though sometimes she didn't have time. We memorised each pellet number and wrote it down later:

Pellet #2804

That's how she would label things in her museum, she said – in which pellet it was found, and on what date, and what it was found with.

In one of the rooms we found a dying-looking creature sitting in an armchair.

He wore a maroon sweatshirt and was missing many feathers. The armchair he sat in was covered in dark gunk, like a pellet, as was the front of his sweatshirt. He was glued to the chair by his pellet mess.

He wore huge plastic glasses that were so dirty we couldn't see his eyes, and luckily he could not see us, but he could hear us and he let out a feeble, 'Hoo.'

We moved a piece of furniture in front of the door of the room he was in, just in case.

'How did he get inside?' I asked Susan.

'He must have hatched in here,' she said.

His wings looked all crumpled and broken in the sweatshirt; it was too small for him.

'How did he get in? The windows are small, Susan.' I trembled and tried to clutch Susan but she pushed me away.

'Maybe someone brought the egg in. Maybe they were going to eat the egg and it hatched, or they planned on raising the creature thinking it would be their friend, but the creature ate them, in the end,' she said.

'What are we going to do, Susan?' I cried.

She said, 'I'll do something.'

I went back to our room and read *Jane Eyre*, which Susan had given me.

Later, I leaned out of the window. I was small but it was still very tight – the window was even smaller than the ones on the first floor. The creature was nailed to the door. Its glasses were tied to its face so they wouldn't fall off and its body was nailed so the wings were spread out, each wing with a nail in it. I wondered why she hadn't kept the creature for the museum, to display along with all the objects; why she hadn't sliced it open for us to study. I had never seen a creature up close before – we were always looking and running away from them, frying pans held high. I wanted to see what they looked like inside.

I got used to eating live mice, they were warm and didn't need to be cooked. I stuck them in my mouth, head first, and never when Susan was looking, though she told me my poo smelled worse. She liked the help with cleaning. It wasn't good to have a museum full of mice, they'd eat her objects, and worst of all, Maud's jumper. The rats were too big, too big for me to eat. Whenever we caught one we threw it out of the window. They screamed as they fell and ran back towards the building if they survived.

At night we could hear woohoohoo all around – they could hear the scuttling and scratching of the mice, but they couldn't get in.

Once you ate a mouse live, it was hard to think of eating them dead again.

Whenever I grabbed one, Susan asked, 'Do you want to boil that dirty thing?' before I ate it.

We went out each day, at noon. We went out of another door we found, on the side of the building, which was not as large as the front door where Susan had stuck the creature.

We went past a huge old building with a hole in its side, from which large sticks of metal stuck out. 'That's the *old* museum,' said Susan. She wanted to explore it, but there were too many creatures with burrows in there. There were pellets thrown up all around it. We found pieces of amber with very ancient insects in them. We found teeth. We found a whole tin of brown sugar in a pellet; there was a picture of a girl on the tin, which is why they'd swallowed it whole, but the tin was safe and unopened in the pellet, and the sugar tasted fine. We found in one a figure of a man wearing an outfit with a diamond-patterned shape on it, in green, black and yellow. He was missing an arm and his head, 'But he was most definitely a man,' said Susan. 'See again, they try and eat things like this because it's made to look like something that's alive. They're stupid.'

She spat on a rag and polished it. In another pellet was a ton of string and a human skull. 'Is that Maud's skull?' I asked.

'It's not Maud's skull,' said Susan. 'I knew Maud's head very well, it was much larger than this.' Still, she boiled the skull in her kettle till it was clean, then put it on the mantelpiece.

Medical students must have put skulls on the mantelpiece, too, while living here, she said. She liked the skull for company because it was older than me.

Maud, Maud, Maud, Susan said in her sleep every night. If she couldn't sleep, she sat there in the dark saying Maud, Maud, Maud, sometimes in a growl: 'Maud.'

I had dreams, too – I dreamed the creatures spoke, though the words were very strange and I hadn't heard them before. I tried visualising them in my head: KORE, GUNAIKA. I asked Susan. 'They don't have a language,' she said, 'they just hoowoohoo.'

There was a large house with a huge golden Σιγμα on it, near our new home, the roof all splattered with white.

Susan held up her frying pan behind her head. 'What is that, Susan?' I asked.

'I don't know.'

I turned the Σ round and round in my head. It felt like a metal tool or trinket of some sort. I kept asking about it until Susan said, 'You will stay at home and clean while I go and look for Maud and things to put in my museum. And read your books, too.'

We found all sorts of books in our future museum. There were more books left with words than images, because the creatures went after images. Susan taught me to read and made me read quite a lot of books: whatever she could find. I read until Susan came home and took an arm and a hand bone out of her bag.

'Is that Maud's arm?' I asked.

'I would let you know if it was Maud's – in fact, it would be clear from my behaviour if it was Maud's,' she said.

We ate sugar and cleaned the room next to ours. We cleaned up all the mouse droppings and I got to eat a mouse whenever I grabbed one. I didn't like to eat the tails; I accumulated them in my pocket then threw them out of the window.

Susan gave me her bags of tiny bones to sort through, and a bottle of glue. She wanted to display skeletons of all sorts in our museum. I thought I could kill a mouse to see how to assemble a rodent skeleton – the bones got all mixed up in a pellet – but as soon as Susan went out again, I pushed a chair to the window of our room and watched the park, instead of reading or cleaning or preparing our museum. I only took breaks to eat mice, swallowing them whole. I kept forgetting to dissect one and see its bones. I was just too hungry. My stomach felt sick, but I kept on grabbing and eating. Once in a while a creature, out in the daytime desperate with hunger, would fly by, white, brown, talons. Sometimes they slept in the park trees, slightly moving now and then, throwing up pellets which fell down from trees with a plump. Susan always stopped to open them.

It was a hungry daytime one that got Susan. She was coming home to me with a large bag. I saw her! Susan!

All her things fell – plop, plop, her various bags – as she was carried away. An odd-shaped skull and a kettle rolled out of a dropped bag. Things she must have found in a pellet that day. She wasn't screaming, but her body was jerking; she was trying to get out of her jumper, but she was soon too high to drop safely.

I didn't want to see the expression on her face. I looked away. I thought: at least she would find Maud.

Acknowledgements

Thank you: Joanna Lee, Sophie Scard, Kat Aitken, Heather Parry, Kirsty Logan, Heather Palmer, Kirsty Doole, James Roxburgh, Bobby Mostyn-Owen, Brodie Crellin, Anna my mother, Ludwig, Clare Bogen, Oscar Price, everyone at *Bourbon Penn, Extra Teeth, Lifted Brow* and *The White Review*. Special thank you and apologies to Eugene.